Giles Henry Mandeville

**Flushing**

past and present

Giles Henry Mandeville

**Flushing**
*past and present*

ISBN/EAN: 9783337369279

Printed in Europe, USA, Canada, Australia, Japan

Cover: Foto ©Andreas Hilbeck / pixelio.de

More available books at **www.hansebooks.com**

# PAST AND PRESENT:

## A HISTORICAL SKETCH,

BY

### REV. G. HENRY MANDEVILLE,

OF NEWBURG, N. Y.

FORMER PASTOR OF THE PROTESTANT REFORMED
DUTCH CHURCH, AT FLUSHING.

———◄◆►———

FLUSHING, L. I.
PUBLISHED BY THE HOME LECTURE COMMITTEE OF 1857–8.
———
1860.

# CONTENTS.

# LIST OF ILLUSTRATIONS.

THE FOX OAKS.

FRIENDS' MEETING HOUSE.

St. GEORGE'S CHURCH.

METHODIST EPISCOPAL CHURCH.

REFORMED DUTCH CHURCH.

CONGREGATIONAL CHURCH.

St. MICHAEL'S ROMAN CATHOLIC CHURCH.

SANDFORD HALL.

FLUSHING INSTITUTE.

FLUSHING FEMALE INSTITUTE.

# CORRESPONDENCE.

Rev. G. H. Mandeville,

   Dear Sir,—At the conclusion of the course of Lectures for the benefit of the village Poor, the following resolution, offered by Gen. Allan Macdonald, was unanimously adopted:

"*Resolved*, That the thanks of the audience be presented to the Rev. G. H. Mandeville, for his interesting Lecture on Flushing, and that he be requested to furnish the Committee with a copy of the same for publication."

In communicating the wishes of the audience permit us to add our personal solicitation, and hope that you will comply with the request.

     Very Respectfully,

      Geo. C. Baker, *Chairman*,

Joseph H. Vedder, *Secretary*.

*Committee.*—Allan P. Northrup, J. W. Barstow and E. M. Griswold.

  Flushing, March 22d, 1858

—

*Messrs. G. C. Baker, A. P. Northrup, J. W. Barstow, M. D., E. M. Griswold, Joseph H. Vedder, M. D.*, Committee, &c.

  Gentlemen,

   Your note of March 22d, 1858, was duly received and appreciated. In accordance with the request it contains, I now place in your hands my little loaf of home-made bread. You may think it has been a long time in baking. True, yet not so long as it would have been, but for my removal from the village. Had I continued to reside in your midst I should in all likelihood have further prosecuted my investigations, and gathered additional items of interest. But my change of residence has rendered this labor exceedingly inconvenient, and I therefore conclude to give you what material I have. It is not as perfect as I could desire, or as it might be made with longer time. It makes no pretension to *perfection* either in manner or matter. It is simply a small contribution to a valuable local history hitherto unwritten. It is as reliable and as full as I could make it with the materials at command. I have not made a single statement for which I did not believe the authority sufficient. If on any subject I have been misinformed, or if I make statements not founded in truth, it is not because diligent, honest endeavors have not been made to ascertain the facts. My long delay in placing the manuscripts in your hands must be attributed, in part, to my desire to secure correctness, and obtain *all* that was reliable in our history—and *in part also* to the numerous and long interruptions to which I am necessarily subject by the duties of my calling.

As the lecture was originally prepared merely for delivery, the authority for each separate statement was not noted at the time; and cannot now be fixed without considerable labor. I prefer therefore, to name in this place, the sources whence I have drawn the materials which I have endeavored to weave together in the following narrative: "Documents relating to the Colonial History of the Sate of New York;" "Broadhead's Colonial History;" "Thompson's History of Long Island;" "Onderdonk's Queens County Incidents;" "Census of the Sate of New York for 1855;" also data of manuscript furnished by Rev. J. Carpenter Smith, of St. George's Church, Flushing; MSS. belonging to the Bowne family; MSS. of Henry Onderdonk, Jr., of Jamaica; MSS. in possession of Robert Townsend, Esq., of Albany; MSS.

in possession of Rev. F. L. Hawks, D. D. LL. D., of New York; and items furnished by James Riker, Jr. author of of the History of Newtown, L. I. To all of these gentlemen I would make grateful acknowledgments of obligation for their courtesy, kindness and assistance. I would also express my thanks to those of our citizens who have in any wise aided me in this matter.

I can not omit to make my most thankful obligations to the gentlemen of the Committee; and especially to Mr. Geo. C. Baker and to Joseph H. Vedder, M. D., for their courteous treatment and very valuable assistance.

If this effort may but serve to stimulate enquiry and effort in this direction on the part of some one better qualified and having more leisure for the work than myself, I shall feel abundantly repaid for my labor. I should be very much gratified to see a full and perfect history of your village, in which I have spent eight of the best years of my life in honest and prayerful labors for its welfare—with which are connected some of my pleasantest associations and of whose inhabitants there are not a few whom I rejoice to call my " friends."

As my manuscript was mainly written previously to my removal, I have retained throughout the first personal pronoun " *our*" instead of changing it to the second " *your*."

With these few explanatory remarks, by way of preface, I commit the MSS to your hands,

With much esteem, I am,

Yours, very respectfully,

G. HENRY MANDEVILLE.

*Head Quarters' Parsonage,*
*Newburgh, Dec. 17th,* 1859.

# CHAPTER I.

The work of the historical chronicler is a work
of severe toil. No one, unaccustomed to researches
of this kind, can form an adequate conception of
the difficulty and labor of collecting, arranging
and connecting materials so as to form an interesting and instructive narrative. Although this
volume is small and unpretending, yet the labor
of preparing it has been far greater than its, size
indicates. The chief difficulty has arisen from
the fact that the records of the town have been
destroyed. They were kept in the residence of
John Vanderbilt, Town Clerk. In October, 1789,
his house, with the Records, was consumed by fire.
*Nelly*, a slave of D. Braine, and *Sarah*, a slave of
J. Vanderbilt were the *incendiaries*. They were
brought to trial; Nelly was convicted as principal,
and Sarah as accessory before the fact. Both
were sentenced to be hung on the 15th of October, 1790.

By this calamity we were deprived of those
sources of full and authentic information in refer-

2

ence to the earlier history of our town which most other towns have preserved. Hence we are necessitated to glean such facts as have dropped from official documents, private letters, and traditional reports. With these, scanty as they are, and only sufficient to whet the appetite of the hungry searcher after antiquarian lore, we must be content.

The place began to be settled about 1643—4. The first settlers, were not Hollanders, as many, I find, suppose, but English; although doubtless both Holland and French emigrants soon settled among them. They fled from England to Holland, because they could not enjoy religious freedom in their own land, and Holland was then the asylum for the oppressed of all lands. They named their settlement "*Vlissingen*," after a town of the same name in Holland. This, in after years, was anglicized into "*Flushing*."

In the "Remonstrance of New Netherland to the States General of the United Netherlands," which is dated the 28th of July, 1649, Long Island is called "a crown of the province by reason of its great advantage of excellent bays and harbors as well as convenient and fertile land"— Among its towns is one named "Flushing, which is a *handsome* village and tolerably stocked with cattle." Our village, by this evidence, was renowned, even in olden time, for its beauty and thrift.

The settlers were, many of them, men of some means. It was not so however with all. Some were compelled to sell their services after their arrival to pay for their passage hither. As illustrative of this we find among the papers in possesion of the Bowne family the following contract :

" It is contracted between John Bowne, inhabitant in Flushing, in ye province of New Netherlands, in America, on ye one part, and *James Clement of ye Buthrop-Bridge of Durham, in ye kingdom of England, on ye other part. That is to say, that ye sayd James Clement do hereby bind and obligate myself to ye most of my power truly and faithfully to serve ye sayd John Bowne, his heirs and assigns, ye full term of six years after my arrival at ye habitation of ye sayd John Bowne, and to pay one-half of my freight or passage from ye place of embarkation to ye place of ye aforesaid mansion. In performance of ye promise by ye sayd James Clement ye aforesaid John Bowne do hereby bind and obligate myself, heirs and assigns to pay or cause to be paid to ye said James Clement ye full quantity of two hun-

---

*On the list of inhabitants for the year 1693 occurs the name of James Clement—probably this very man.

dred and forty pound weight of Tobacco, and sufficient to clothe him with two suits of Apparell, one fit to Labor, ye other fit to use on other occasions. JOHN BOWNE,
JAMES CLEMENT.

John Lodge, *Witness.*
Sylvanus Halford, *Witness.*
*Amsterdam, in Holland,*
*the* 30*th day of the* 5*th mo.,* 1663, *new style.*

They were men of courage to face and overcome difficulties and hardships, incident to their situation in a new settlement, in a new country.

They were men of noble spirit. They were not afraid nor ashamed to work with their own hands. Labor was not considered a disgrace. The plebeian-touch of a poor man was not a contamination. To work, even in the service of another, was not a sign of inferiority, intellectually or socially. We find accordingly that this very John Bowne, who was one of the largest land proprietors, and should be reckoned among the wealthiest in those days of democratic simplicity,—honestly makes this record in his journal: "Monday, Jan'y 7th, 1649, I entered into Mr. Phillip's service, for which service I am to have five shillings for every week, one-half in money, and one-half in wine" (he was not then a Friend) " to myself or whom I

ST GEORGES EPISCOPAL CHURCH

shall assign, and also my diet and lodging and washing, for so long as I shall please to stay with him, I being free at every week's end if I will.

JOHN BOWNE."

It should however be stated, that some doubt has been thrown over the genuineness of this extract—it being a copy and not the original journal. But we conceive that the fact mentioned is entirely characteristic of the men and the times. The very independent nature of the compact shows that it was not a necessity, but a voluntary matter—to be continued only until he should see an opportunity of locating himself permanently upon his own land. To our mind its truth is more probable than its falsity.

*Incorporation.* The first patent of Incorporation of the Town of Flushing was granted by the Dutch Governor, William Keift, and was dated October 10th, 1645. This was renewed under the English authority. The renewal-charter was dated March 24th, 1685 These manuscripts were probably lost in the fire previously noted. The only manuscript the Town has, relative to its Incorporation, is termed an "Exemplification of Flushing Patent." It is dated Feb. 24th, 1792; one hundred and seven years after the renewal by the English, and one hundred and forty-seven years after the original grant by the Dutch autho-

2*

rities. We found it in possession of Capt. George B. Roe, who kindly placed a copy at our disposal. It is only sixty-seven years old, but already many parts are nearly obliterated and can with difficulty be deciphered. Believing its preservation desirable, and that the inhabitants of Flushing would like to read the charter by which they hold their possessions we present it entire. as follows :

" The People of the State of New York, by the Grace of God free and independent : 'To all whom these presents shall come, Send greeting. Know ye that we having inspected the Records remaining in our Secretary's office, Do find there in Book of pattent No. 5, certaine Letters Patent Recorded at the 215 page of the said Book, in the words and figures following. to wit : ' Recorded for the Inhabitants of Flushing, March 24th, 1685. Thomas Dongan, Lieut. Governor and Vice-Admiral of New Yorke, under his Majesty James the Second, by the Grace of God, of England, Scotland, France and Ireland, King, Defender of the Faith, &c., Supreme Lord and Proprietor of the Colony and Province of New York and its Dependencies in America, &c. To all to whom this shall come, Sendeth Greeting— Whereas Richard Nicoll, Esq., formerly Governor General of this Province, under his Royal Highness James, Duke of York and Albany, and of all his Territoryes in America, &c., hath by his certaine writing or patent, bearing date the fifteenth day of February, in the nineteenth year of his Majesty's Reigne, Anno. Dom. one thousand six hundred and sixty-six, given and granted unto John Lawrence, Alderman of the Citty of New York, Richard Cornell, Charles Bridges, William Lawrence, Robert Terry, William Noble, John Forbush, Elias Doughty, Robert Field, Edward Farrington, John Marston, Anthony Field, Phillip Udall, Thomas Stiles, Benjamin Field, William Pidgeon, John Adams, John Hinchman, Nicholas Parcell, Tobias Feakes and John Bowne, as Pattentees for and in the behalf of themselves and their Associates, the Freeholders and Inhabitants of the Town of Flushing, their heirs, successors and Inhabitants for ever, ALL that certaine Town in the North Riding of Yorkshire, upon Long Island, called by the name of Flushing, Scituate lying and being in the north side of the said island; which said hath a certaine tract of land belonging thereunto, and bounded westward beginning at the mouth of a creeke upon the East River, known by the name of Flushing Creeke, and from thence including a certain neck of land called Tuesneck, to run Eastward as far as Matthew Garretson's Bay, from the head or middle whereof a Line is to be run South East, in length about three miles and about two miles in breadth, as the Land hath been surveyed and laid out by virtue of an order made at the General Meeting, held at the town of Hemstead, in the month of March, one thousand six hundred and sixty-four; then that theire may be the same lattitude in Breadth on the South side as on the North, to run in two direct lines Southward to the middle of the hills as is directed by another order made of the Generall Meeting aforesaid, which passing East and West, as the two are now markt is the Bounds between the said Towns of Flushing and Jamaica, for the greatest parte of which said tract of Land and premissess there was heretofore a Pattent Granted from the Dutch Governor, William Keift, bearing date the tenth day of October, one thousand six hundred and forty-five, stilo novo, unto Thomas Farrington, John Lawrence, John Hicks, and divers others pattentees, their successors, associates and assignees, for them to improve, manure and settle a competent number of familyes thereupon, as by the said pattent remaining upon Record in the Secretary's office, relacion being thereto had, may fully and att large appeare ; and whereas for a further strengthening of the aforesaid Title and peaceable enjoyment of the premissess, and to take away utterly and destroy all cause, matters and pretences of controversie or variance that might

at any time arise from Tackaponshee, Sachem
Quassauwascoe, Suscananian, Rumsuck, and We-
rah, Catharum, Nimham, Shuntheweban, Ninhan's
Soune and Oposon Indians, or any other person or
persons whether Christian or Indian, Clajmeing by
from or under them, those following persons deputed by order and on the behalfe of the town of
Flushing : Elias Doughty, Thomas Willett, John
Bowne, Matthias Harvey, Thomas Hicks, Richard Cornell, John Hinchman, Jonathan Wright
and Samuel Hoyt agents of the Freeholders of
the Towne of Flushing, did for and on the Behalfe
of the said Towne in Generall—their Heirs and Associates, by a certain writing or Indenture made,
concluded and confirmed on the fourteenth day of
Aprill, and in the year of our Lord one thousand
six hundred eighty-four, buy and purchase by my
permission and approbacion from the before mencioned Indians" (here follow the same jaw-break-
ing names) " all the lands situate lying and being
on the North Side of Long Island, called and
knowne by the name of Flushing, within Queens
County, the first bounds whereof begin to the
West with Flushing Creeke, to the South by Jamaica Line, to the East by Hemstead Line, and
to the North with the Sound, for and in consideration of a valuable sume then received, before
the signing and sealing of the aforesaid writing

to the full sattisfaceion of the Indians, as by the aforesaid writing or Indenture, relacion thereto being had, dothe more fully and att large appeare. And whereas by articles of agreement dated the sixth day of March, $167\frac{9}{80}$, made between the said Towne of Flushing and Jamaica, the Inhabitants thereof have fully concluded upon a perpetuall Bounds as follows: that from the fott or Bottome of the hills upon the South side the Towne of Jamaica shall have Seven Score Rodd upon a direct or straight Pointe unto the hills in all places from the Eastermost Bounds of Jamaica, being at a marked Walnutt tree, upon Rockie hill, standing upon the west side of the Road be. tween Flushing and Hemstead, to the Westermost Bounds of Jamaica and Flushing in the hills, as by the said agreement, refference being thereto had may fully appeare. And whereas by another certaine writing or agreement dated the last day of June, one thousand six hundred eighty-four, made by Elias Doughty, John Seaman, Thomas Willett and John Jackson, that the Bounds between the Towne of Flushing and Hempstead are to begin at the middle of the Bay where Capt. Jacques runn the line, and to hold the same untill it comes to the land called by the name of the Governor's Land, and then from the South side of the Governor's Land towards the end of the

plaine to the former markt tree that stands in the
Hollow, and to run from thence upon a direct line
unto the Rocky hill Westerly where carts usually
goe to Flushing as by the said agreement relacion being thereto had, may likewise appeare :
and whereas the said Pattentees and their associates the freeholders and Inhabitants of the said
Towne of Flushing hereafter named, have according to the Custom and Practice in this Province
made several divisions, allottments, distinct settlements and improvements of severall pieces and parcells of the above recited tract of Land, within the
limitts abovesaid at their own proper cost and
charge : And whereas applycacion hath been made
to me by Joseph Smith and Jonathan Wright,
persons deputed from the said Towne of Flushing,
for a confirmacion of the aforesaid Tract or parcell
of land and premissess contained in the aforesaid
pattent as it hath since been limited, butted and
bounded by the before mencioned agreement of the
Towne of Flushing with the Townes of Jamaica
and Hemstead ; now for a Confirmacion unto the
present Freeholders and Inhabitants of the said
Towne, their heires and assignes, in the Quiett and
peaceable possession and enjoyment of the aforesaid Tract of Land and premises, KNOW YEE,
that by virtue of the Commission and Authority
unto me given, and power in me residing, I have

ratified, confirmed and granted unto Thomas Willett, John Lawrence Seignor, Elias Doughty, Richard Cornell, Moriss Smith, Charles Morgan, Mary Fleake, Wouter Gisbertson, John Masten, John Cornelis, John Harrison, Denius Holdron, John Hinchman, William Yeates, Joseph Thorne, John Lawrence Junior, Matthias Harveye, Harmanus King, John Farrington, Thomas Williams, Elizabeth Osborne, Joseph Havyland, John Washborne, Aaron Cornelis, John Bowne, William Noble, Samuel Hoyt, Madeline Frances Burto, John Hoper, Thomas Ford, John Jenning, John Embree, Jonathan Wright, Nicholas Parcell, William Lawrence, Richard Townly, Edward Griffin Seignor, David Roe, Richard Tindall, Edward Griffin Junior, John Lawrence at the White Stone, Henry Taylor, Jasper Smith, Richard Wilday, Thomas Townsend, John Thorne, Anthony Field, John Adams, Richard Stockton, James Wittaker, Hugh Copperthwaite, Richard Chew, James Clement, Margaret Stiles, Samuel Thorne, Thomas Hedges, William Haviland, Thomas Hicks, John Terry, David Patrick, James Feake, Thoms Kimacry, Phillip Udall, Thomas Davis, Edward Farrington, Thomas Farrington, Matthew Farrington, John Field, Joseph Hedger, John Talman, William Gaed, William White, Elizabeth Smith, Thomas Partridge,

William Hedger, Benjamin Field, the present
freeholders and Inhabitants of the said Towne
of Flushing, their heires and assignes for ever,
all the before recited tract and Parcell or neck
of land set forth limited and bounded as aforesaid by the aformencioned patent Indian deed of
sale and agreements, together with all and singular the houses, Messuages, Tenements, Fencings,
Buildings, Gardens, Orchards, Trees, Woods, Un-
derwoods, Highways and Easements whatsoever,
belonging or in any wayes appertaining to any of
the afore recited tract, Parcell or neck of land, divisions, Allottments and settlements made and appropriated before the day and the date hereof:
To HAVE AND TO HOLD all the said tract of land
and premissess with theire and every of theire ap-
purtenances to the severall and respective uses
following and to and for no other use, intent, and
purpose whatsoever, that is to say, as for and concerning all and singular the severall and respective
parcells of land and meadow-parte of the grant
ed premissess in any wise taken up, divided, al-
lotted, settled and appropriated before the day of
the date hereof, with the severall and respective
present Inhabitants and Freeholders, Thomas
Willett (here follow the same names last mentioned) to the use and behoof of the said Inhabitants and Freeholders respectively, and theire

3

severall and respective heires and assignes for
ever : And as for and concerning all and every
such parcell or parcells tract or tracts of Land
and Meadow Remainder of the Granted premisses
not yet taken up or appropriated to any particular
person or persons before the day of the date hereof, to the use and behoof of the purchasers above
recited, and to their heires and assignes for ever,
to be equally divided in proportion to the above
recited Inhabitants and Freeholders aforesaid,
and to their respective heires and assignes for
ever without any let, hindrance or molestacion to
be had or reserved upon pretence of joint tenancy
or survivorship or any thing herein contained to
the contrary in any wise notwithstanding : To be
holden of his Most Sacred Majesty, his heires and
successors in free and common succage according
to the tenure of East Greenwich in the Kingdom
of England. Yielding therefore and paying yeare-
ly and every yeare an acknowledgement or quit
rent to his Majesty, his heires and successors as
aforesaid, or to such officer or officers as shall by
him or them be appointed to receive the same at
New Yorke, in lieu of all services and demands
whatsoever *Sixteen* Bushells of good Marchanta-
ble winter Wheate on every five and twentyeth
day of March. IN TESTIMONY whereof I have
caused these presents to be entered upon record

in the Secretarye's office of this Province, and the Seale of the Said Province to be hereunto affixed the 23d day of March, in the yeare of our Lord one thousand six hundred eighty-five, and in the Second yeare of his Majesty's Reigne, &c.

THOMAS DOUGAN, may it please your Honor, The Atturney Generall hath perused this Pattent and finds nothing contained therein prejudiciall to his Majesty's interest.

Examined March 23d, 1685.

JA. GRAHAM.'

"ALL WHICH we have caused to be exemplified by these presents. In testimony whereof we have caused these our Letters to be made patent, and the Great Seal of our State to be hereunto affixed. Witness our truly and well-beloved George Clinton, Esquire, Governor of our Said State, General and Commander in Chief of all the Militia and Admiral of the same, at our City of New York, the twenty-fourth day of February, in the year of our Lord one thousand seven hundred and ninety-two, and in the sixteenth year of our Independence."

The Seal last mentioned is still attached to the document. It is made of wax, covered with paper. It is truly a "*Great* Seal," being ⅝ of an inch in thickness and 3½ inches in diameter. On the outer rim of the one side are stamped the words "The Great Seal of the State of New York." In the centre is a figure designed to represent the rising sun. Underneath is the noble motto of our State—to which may she ever be nobly true in all that enlightens, elevates and blesses her citizens—"Excelsior." On the lower rim of the other side, is the date, in which the *Colony* was transmuted into the *State* of New York, 1777; on the the upper rim the Latin adverb "*frustra*," (in vain); in the centre a huge rock in the midst of the sea, with the waves dashing furiously against it; the whole designed, I suppose, to represent that the State of New York will stand firm as the rock for ever—that the billows of rebellion, revolution and war may dash against it, but to no purpose. They will spend their strength for nought. God of nations, grant that it may be verified to the latest generation! Where is the son of New York who will not respond with a fervent "Amen" to this petition? Nay, where is the son or daughter of these United States that will refuse to pour out this prayer for the whole country—for every State that now is, or may hereafter be incorporated into this wonderful confederacy of Republics, upon which the blessings of Divine Providence have so signally been bestowed. Palsied be the arm that would blot a single "Star" from the galaxy that beautifies our

Country's contstellated Ensign, now blazing forth its radiance to an admiring world!

*Census.*—Exceedingly scanty are the data of early population in the country. The first attempt at Census-taking was made under Governor Dongan, in 1686, who, Oct. 4th, ordered the Sheriff of each county to make reports on or before the 1st of April following. These and all the other statistics give mainly the county totals, not the details of towns and villages. We give below a few of the more prominent and important items as specimens. Each can form his own opinion as to the proportion belonging to Flushing. In Queen's County in

| | Men. | Women. | Children. | Negroes. | Total. |
|---|---|---|---|---|---|
| 1698 ... | 1465. | ...1350.... | 551.... | 199.... | 3565 |

WHITES.

| | Men. | Women. | M. Children. | F Children. | |
|---|---|---|---|---|---|
| 1723 ... | 1568.... | 1599... | 1530... | 1371..... | 6068 |

NEGROES AND OTHER SLAVES.

| | | | | | |
|---|---|---|---|---|---|
| 1723 .... | 393..... | 294.... | 228.... | 208.... | 1123 |

Total, 7191

WHITES.

| | Males above 16. | Females above 16. | Males under 16. | Females under 16. | |
|---|---|---|---|---|---|
| 1749 ... | 1659.... | 1778... | 1630... | 1550.... | 6617 |

BLACKS.

| | | | | | |
|---|---|---|---|---|---|
| 1749 .... | 300..... | 245.... | 429.... | 349.... | 1323 |

Total, 7940

3*

WHITES.

| | Males under 16. | Males above 16. | Females under 16. | Females above 16. | |
|---|---|---|---|---|---|
| 1771 | 1253 | 3033 | 2126 | 2332 | 28744 |

BLACKS.

| | | | | | |
|---|---|---|---|---|---|
| 1771 | 374 | 782 | 545 | 534 | 2235 |

Total, 10,979

| | Electors owning Freeholds, worth £100 & over. | worth from £20 to £100. | Electors not freeholders, renting tenements of annual value of 40s. |
|---|---|---|---|
| 1790 | 1274 | 1397 | 438 |
| 1795 | 1372 | 303 | 557 |
| 1801 | 1659 | 158 | 558 |

| | worth $250 & over. | worth from $60 to $250. | annual value of $5. | other free male citizens. |
|---|---|---|---|---|
| 1821 | 2080 | 254 | 814 | 1067 |

Valuation of estates in the Town of Flushing, 1675, October 9th:

| Negeres. | Acres Land. | Meadow. | Horses. | Oxen. | Cows. | Swine. | Sheep. |
|---|---|---|---|---|---|---|---|
| 19 | 151 | 441 | 59 | 7 | 180 | 103 | 391 |

Rate, £18 3s. 10d.

September 29th, 1683, the total of Flushing estimates amounted to £26 15s. 10d.

Slaves in Queen's County, in years

| 1790 | 1800 | 1810 | 1814 | 1820 |
|---|---|---|---|---|
| 2039 | 1528 | 809 | 630 | 559 |

In 1817, March 31st, the Act was passed freeing the slaves born after July 4th, 1797—males at 28, females at 25 years of age. Every child born after the passage of the Act was free at 21.

# Comparative population of the Town of Flushing.

| 1790 | 1800 | 1810 | 1814 | 1830 | 1840 | 1850 | 1855 |
|------|------|------|------|------|------|------|------|
| 1607 | 1818 | 2230 | 2271 | 2820 | 4124 | 5376 | 7970 |

## The classification for 1855 is as follows:

| WHITES. | | BLACKS. | |
|---------|---------|---------|---------|
| Males, | Females, | Males. | Females. |
| 3699 | 3734 | 260 | 277 |

| | | | | | Voters. |
|--------|---------|----------|---------|---------|-------------|
| Single, | Married, | Widowers, | Widows, | Natives, | Naturalized, |
| 4834 | 2865 | 74 | 197 | 781 | 444 |

| Aliens, | No. of families, | Owners of land, | Over 21 years not able to read or write, | Over 21 years can read but not write, |
|---------|-----------------|-----------------|------------------------------------------|--------------------------------------|
| 1943 | 1500 | 657 | 338 | 154 |

The population of the village of Flushing, was in

1855...................................3488

Whitestone, ...........................630

Strattonport. ........................1150

## Agricultural Statistics for 1855.

| | Bushels harvested. | No. of Acres, |
|-----------------|--------------------|---------------|
| Winter Wheat, | 141191 | — |
| Oats, | 20763 | 879 |
| Rye, | 4195 | 289 |
| Barley, | 580 | 24 |
| Buckwheat, | 1864 | 262 |
| Corn, | 42476 | $1359\frac{1}{4}$ |
| Potatoes, | 36489 | $975\frac{5}{8}$ |

---

In the appendix we have given a list of families in Flushing, (including English, Dutch and French) from 1645 to 1698, gathered from various old records and documents, by Henry Onderdonk, Jr., of Jamaica, L. I.

# CHAPTER II.

INDIANS—INDIAN TITLE—COLONIAL INCIDENTS, &c.

The tribe of Indians which inhabited this section of the Island was the Matinecock. It was very numerous, and claimed jurisdiction over the lands "East of Newtown as far as the West line of Smithtown." Large banks of clam and oyster shells are still to be seen in several localites—showing that they were not strangers to the esculent properties of a good "bake," or a fine "fry." "The Wampum" made in this section of the Island was considered superior to any in circulation among the Indians. Stone and other hatchets and tomahawks have been found in several sections and are in possession of some of our citizens.

When land was purchased from the Indians, the price paid them was *one axe* for fifty acres. Wampum, passing as money, was the only circulating medium. Tradition reports that once upon a time an *English Shilling* was found about a mile from the landing, on the road to Manhasset. Whence could it have come? Who could have lost so unusual a possession? One tradition says, that after considerable difficulty it was traced to an English peddler who had passed through the place; another traces its ownership to a person

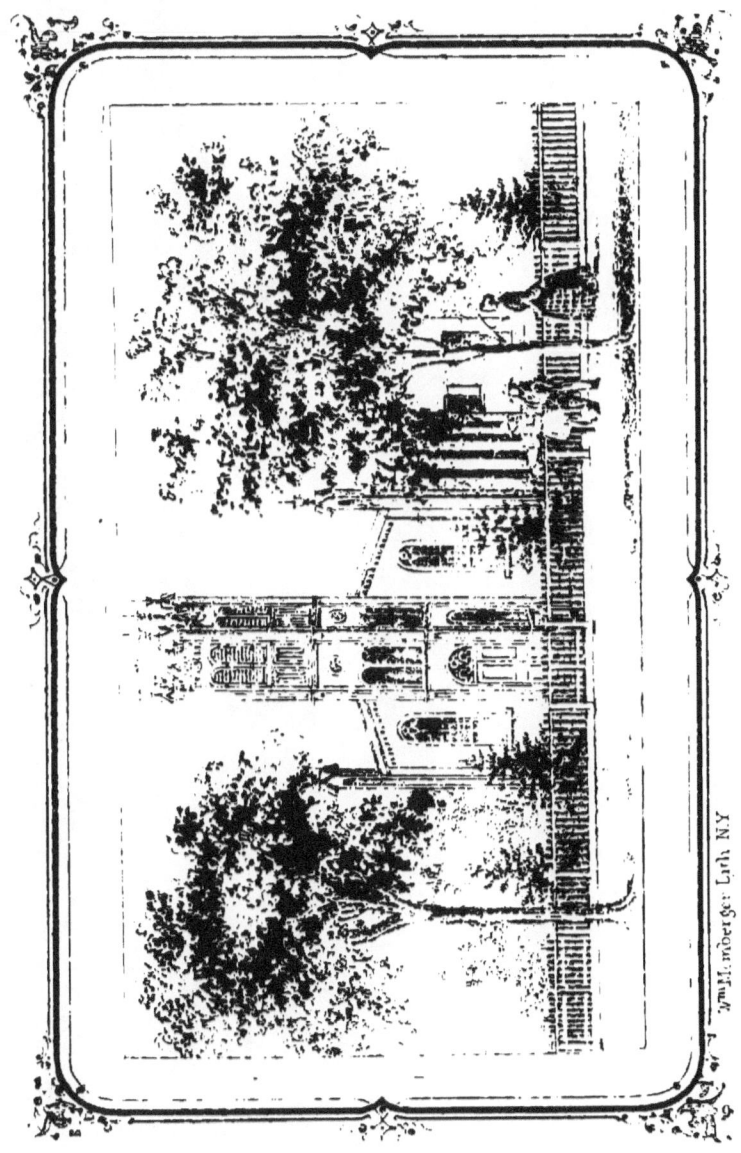

METHODIST EPISCOPAL CHURCH

Wm Mandenger Lith N.Y

who kept a small store at the head of the bay.
This latter individual also owned a large boat
which he had purchased from the Indians, and
which would carry a hogshead of molasses, and
three or four passengers, and with which he made
voyages to and from New Amsterdam.

The last *Indian grant* of Flushing, was made
April 14th, 1684. An indenture between "Sack-
apowsha" and other Indians, "the true owners
and proprietors of all the lands scituate, &c." called Flushing, "sell for good reasons, &c." the
same "unto Elias Doughty, Thomas Willett, John
Bowne, Matthyas Harvey, Thomas Hickes, Richard Cornell, John Hinchman, Jonathan Wright
and Samuel Hoyt," the agents of the freeholders
of the said town—"the Indians reserve the privi-
ledge of cutting *bulrushes forever* within the said
tract."

April 10th, 1693. The name of Long Island
was altered to the "Island of Nassau." This
change was made from motives of political vanity.
The name was never explicitly repealed; yet it
was never a popular favorite and gradually *was
dropped and became obsolete.*

After the re-capture by the Dutch, in 1673, at
a meeting of Council of War, "holden in Fort
William Hendrick, the 13th of August, A. D.,
1673," the five English towns, Flushing Heem-

stede, Rustdorp or Jamaica, Middelborg or Newtown, and Oysterbay, "were summoned and ordered to submit to their High Mightinesses, the
Lords States-General of the United Netherlands,
and His Serene Highness the Prince of Orange,
etc., and to send hither immediately their Deputies, together with their Constable's staves and
English flags, when they would, as circumstances
permit, be furnished with Prince's flags instead of
those of the English."

August 22d. The Deputies of Flushing appeared, handed in "one flag and one Constable's staff,"
and also presented a petition wherein they declare
their submission, &c., whereupon it was resolved
that "the same privileges and rights which are
given to the inhabitants and subjects of the Dutch
nation shall, in like manner, be granted and allowed them, &c."—"with this warning, nevertheless,
that the petitioners shall in future demean them-
seves as loyal subjects, and attempt in nowise, as
some have formerly done, contrary to honor and
oath, for which they are now pardoned on their
request and submission, to take up arms against
this government, under the penalty that the
transgressors shall, without any mercy or favor,
be totally ruined and punished as they deserve."

The five towns were also ordered " to cause to be
nominated by their Commonalty, and to present

the names of three persons for Schout, and three for Secretary, and six persons for Magistrates" for each town.

At a meeting of Council, 31st August, the following were elected for the five towns:

For Schout—William Lawrence,

" Secretary—Casel Van Brugge.

For Schepens of Flushing:

John Hingsman,  ⎱
Francis Bloetgoet,  ⎰ Sworn the 4th of
Richard Wildie,  ⎰ September, 1673.

August 29th was adopted the following form of oath, " to be taken by the inhabitants of the English Nation :"

" We do sware in the presence of the Almighty God, tthat wee shall be true and faithfull to the the United Provinces of his Serene Highnesse the Highand Mighty Lords. the Staets Gennerall of Lord Prince of Orange, and to their Governors here for the tÿme being, and to behave orselves uppon all occasions, as true and lawfull subjects, provided onlÿ, that wee shall not be forced in armes against our owne nation if they be sent bÿ authority of his Majesty of England, except they be accompanied by a commission of force of other nations when wee do oblidge orselves to take up arms against them, So help us God."

Capt. Knyff, Lieut. Hubert and Clerk Hermans

were commissioned to administer the Oath, and on Sept. 22d, they reported :

"Flushing 67 men, 51 of whom have taken the oath ; the remainder absent, are ordered as above—(that is to take the oath before the Schout or Secretary.)  Among these are twenty Dutch."

Gov. Colve, "this 21st Xber, 1673," addresses a letter to William Lawrence, to be communicated to the five English towns.  In this, after stating that he had made a visit to some of the Dutch towns and regretting that want of time prevented his doing so to the others, he says: "Wherefore I have thought fitt to salute you by these Lines, and witthall to recommend unto you as you wish the welfare and tranquility of yourselves to be true and faithfull according to your Oaths and Promises, and not to be deluded by any Illminded Spirits, as some of the Eastern Townes very unwisely have falsified the same, whom due tyme as rebellious will reipe the fruit thereof.  You are also Required to take care that good order be kept in your Respective Townes, and if any thing should be attempted by any in prejudice to ye government in generall, or any of your Townes in Particular to give me Imediate Notice thereof not doubting with ye help & assistance of God, fully to maintaine all true Subjects in their Rights and privileges against all them that shall attempt any thing in prejudice of the same. Soe Recommending you to ye protextion of ye almighty God. I rest.

Your Loving ffriend."

Jan'y 17th, 1648. John Townsend, Edward (Hart, ?) Thomas Styles, John Lawrence and John Hicks were summoned to appear before Gov. Stuyvesant and Council, on Jan'y 23d, as the principal persons who resist the Dutch mode of choosing Sheriff, "pretending it is against the adopted course in the Fatherland"—and who refuse to contribute their share of the maintenance of the " christian, pious, reformed Minister ;" and if they refuse, to be apprehended and prosecuted by the Attorney General.

This is the first symptom of positive resistance to the authority of the Dutch Governor. It had been agitating for sometime, and continued to foment afterwards. It directed itself with peculiar emphasis against the endeavor to enforce conformity to the State church. Although religious liberty was the glory of the Fatherland, was especially provided for and guaranteed in the colonial charters and was commanded upon the Governors, still these latter magnates, in the exercise of their " brief authority," disregarded these enactments and attempted to cöerce the consciences of their subjects. As in New England among the Puritans, so in New Netherlands among the Dutch, the Quakers, then a new and growing sect, were the objects of especial dislike and persecution. Not a few of the inhabitants of Flushing were subjected to sufferings for conscience sake. Among others Henry Townsend, Sept. 15th, 1657, was condemned in *an amende of £8 Flanders*, or else to depart from the province within six weeks, for having called together *conventicles*. This at once aroused the people of Flushing and Jamaica, and they assembled and addressed the following spirited document to the Governor :

" *Remonstrance of Inhabitants of Flushing and Jamaica, to Gov. Stuyvesant.*

" Right Honorable—You have been pleased to send up unto us a certain prohibition or command that we should not retaine or entertaine any of those people called Quakers, because they are supposed to be by some, seducers of the people. For our part we cannot condemn them in this case, neither can we stretch out our hands against them, to punish, banish or persecute them, for out of Christ God is a consuming fire, and it is a fearful thing to fall into the hands of the living God.

Wee desire therefore in this case not to judge least we be judged, neither to condemn least we

be condemned, but rather let every man stand or
fall to his own Maister. Wee are commande by
the Law to doe good unto all men, especially to
those of *the household of Faith*. And though for
the present we seem to be insensible of the law
and the Lawgiver, yet when death and the law
assault us, if wee have our advocake to seeke,
who shall plead for us in this case of conscience
betwixt God and our own souls, the powers of this
world can neither assist us, neither excuse us,
for if God justifye who can condemn; and if God
condemn there is none can justifye. And for those
jealousies and suspicions which some have of
them, that they are destructive unto Magistracy
& Ministerye, (this) can not bee, for the magistrate hath the sword in his hand, and the minister
hath the sword in his hand—as witnesse those two
great examples which all magistrates and minis
ters are to follow, (Moses) and Christ, whom God
raised up maintained and defended against all
the enemies both of Flesh and Spirit; and therefore that which is of God will stand, and that
which is of man will come to nothing. And as
the Lorde hath taught Moses or the civil powers
to give an outward liberty in the state by the law
written in his hearte for the good of all, and can
truly judge who is good, who is evil, who is true,
and who is false, and can pass definite sentence of

life or death against that man which rises up against
the fundamental law of the States General. Soe he
hath made his ministers a savour of life unto life,
and a savour of death unto death. The laws of
*Love, Peace and Liberty* in the state extending to
*Jews, Turks and Egyptians,* as they are considered
*the sonnes of Adam,* which is the glory of the outward state of Holland, soe Love, Peace and Liberty,
extending to all in Christ Jesus, condemns hatred,
War and Bondage. And because our Saviour
saith it is impossible but that offences will come,
but woe unto him by whom they cometh, our desire is not to offend one of his little ones, in whatsoever form, name or title hee appears in, whether
Presbyterian, Independent, Baptist or Quaker, but
shall be glad to see any thing of God in any of
them, desiring to doe unto all men, as wee desire
that all men should doe unto us, which is the true
law both of church and state; for our Saviour
saith this is the law and the prophets. Therefore
if any of these said persons come in love unto us,
we *cannot in conscience lay violent hands upon them,*
but give them free egresse and regresse into our
Town and house, as God shall persuade our consciences. And in this we are true subjects both
of *church* and *state,* for we are bounde by the law
of God and man to doe good unto all men and
evil to noe man. And this is according to the pat-

tent and charter of our Towne, given unto us in
the name of the States Generall, which we are
not willing to infringe and violate, but shall houlde
to our pattent and shall remaine your humble subjects, the inhabitants of Vlissengen,—Written this
27th of December, in the year 1657, by mee,

EDWARD HART, *Clerk.*

Tobias Feake,
William Noble,
Nicholas Parsell,
William Thorne, *Seignior,*
Michael Milner,
William Thorne, Junior,
Henry Townsend,
Nicholas Blackford,
George Wright,
Edward Tark,
John Foard,
Mirabel fre,
Henry Bamtell,
John Stour,
Nathaniel (Coles ?)
Benjamin Hubbard,
Fdward Hart,
John Maidon,
John Townsend,
Edward Farrington,

4*

Philip Ed,
William Pidgion,
George Blee, (?)
Elias Doughtie,
Antonie Field,
Richard Horton,
Edward Griffin,
Nathaniel (Coe, ?)
Robert Field, Seinor,
Robert Field, Junior.
Tobias Feake, the Sheriff."

But it was of no avail. The sturdy old Dutch Governor was unrelenting. The persecution against the Quakers was persevered in with increasing violence. The Sheriff, delivering the document, was immediately arrested by order of Stuyvesant, by Nicassius De Sille, his Attorney General. Farrington and Noble, two of the signers, and also Magistrates were likewise arrested and imprisoned. Hart, who admitted writing the document as embodying the sentiments of a village meeting held at the house of Michael Milnor, was also thrown into prison. John Townsend, who then resided at Rusdorp or Jamaica, was summoned Jan. 10th, 1658, and being asked if he had been with Hart to persuade Farrington to sign the remonstrance, answered that he had been at Flushing, and visited Farrington as an old ac quaintance; also that "he had been at Gravesend but not in company with the banished female Quaker." Yet, as the Court were *suspicious* that he *favored* the Quakers, he was held to bail to appear when summoned, in the sum of £12. Henry Townsend was again brought before the Council, Jan. 15th, 1658, was fined £100 Flanders, for treating with contempt the placards of the Director, for lodging Quakers again and again, "which he unconditionally confessed," "and so to remain arrested till the said amende be paid, besides the costs and mises of justice." Sheriff Feake, "maintaining that all sects, and principally the aforesaid heretical and abominable sect of Quakers, shall or ought to be tolerated, which is directly contrary to the aforesaid orders and placards of the director General and Council," was degraded from his office, and sentenced to be banished from the province, or to pay an amende of two hundred guilders.

Jan. 10th. Farrington and Noble presented the following written confession:

"To the Honorable the governor and his Council, the humble petition of William Noble and Edward Farrington,

" *Sheweth*, That, whereas your petitioners having subscribed a writing offensive to your honors, presented by Tobias Feake, we acknowledge our offence for acting so inconsiderately, and humbly crave your pardon, promising, for the time to come, that we shall *offend* no more in that kind, And your petitioners shall ever pray for your health and happiness.

WILLIAM NOBLE,
EDWARD FARRINGTON."

In consideration of this and their *verbal* confession to being *seduced* and *inveigled* by Feake, their fault was *graciously pardoned and forgiven*, on payment of costs of examination.

The following was also presented :

"Right Honorable governor and Council;— Forasmuch as I have written a writing whereat you take offence, my humble desire is, that your Honors would be favorable and gracious to me, for it was not written in disobedience unto any of your laws; therefore my humble request is for your mercy, not your judgment; and that you would be pleased to consider my poor estate and condition, and relieve me from my bonds and imprisonment, and I shall endeavor hereafter, to walk inoffensively unto your lordships, and shall ever remain your humble servant to command.

EDWARD HART."

Whereupon the following action was taken :—
"1658, 23d Jan'y : Being presented and read, the

petition of Edward Hart, clerk of Vlissingen, and considered his promises that he would conduct himself more prudently, and the intercessions of several of the inhabitants of said village, that he always was willing to serve his neighbors, and that, as one of the oldest inhabitants, he was thoroughly acquainted with their affairs : and further, that the Sheriff, Tobias Feeke, advised him to draw the aforesaid remonstrance of the first of January, and then presented : and further, that he has a large family to maintain ; so is it, that the director general and Council pardoned his fault for this time, provided that he pay the expenses and misses of judgment."

Other instances of this bitter persecution of Quakers will be noted in subsequent parts of this volume. Many were arrested and prosecuted for *adultery*, because, although married according to the simple requirements of the Quaker faith, they had not complied with the formularies of the religion of the State. Notwithstanding repeated injunctions from the Fatherland, Stuyvesant continued his opposition throughout his term of office. In 1661 an ordinance was passed, providing, "that besides the reformed religion, no *Conventicles* should be holden in *houses*, *barnes*, *ships*, *woods* or *fields*, under the penalty of fifty guilders for each person, man, woman or child, attending for the first offence; double for the second; quadruple for the third; and arbitrary correction for every other."

But the Dutch Governor Stuyvesant was not the only persecutor of the Quakers in New Netherlands. Under the English authority, during the administration of Lord Cornbury, religious intolerence equally tyrannical was manifested towards all denominations except the Episcopal. A noted example of Quaker persecution, that of Samuel Bownas, will be more fully narrated in a subsequent chapter.

We find the following extraordinary record:

" April 8th, 1648. Thomas Hall, an inhabitant of fflishingen, in New Netherlands, being accused that he prevented the Sheriff of fflishingen to doe his duty, and execute his office, in apprehending Thomas Heyes, which Thomas Hall confesseth, *that he kept the door shut*, so that noe one might assist the Sheriff, demands mercy, and promise *he will do it never again*, and *regrets very much* that he did so. The director general and council doing justice condemn the said Thomas Hall in a fine of 25 guilders, to be applied at the discretion of the council."

" April 22d 1655, Thomas Saul, William Lawrence and Edward Farrington were appointed Magistrates from a list of persons nominated by

the Town; and Tobias Feeke was appointed
Sheriff."

Town meetings were forbidden, "except for
highly interesting and pressing reasons;" and

" March, 26th, 1658, it was resolved to change
the municipal government of Flushing. In this
document, after formally pardoning the Town for
its mutinous orders and resolutions, Gov. Stuyvesant says, 'in future I shall appoint a Sheriff,
acquainted not only with the English and Dutch
languages, but with Dutch practical law; and that
in future there shall be chosen seven of the most
reasonable and respectable of the inhabitants, to
be called tribunes and townsmen; and whom the
Sheriff and Magistrates shall consult in all cases;
and that a tax of twelve stivers per morgen is
laid on the inhabitants for the support of an orthodox minister; and such as do not sign a written
submission to the same, in six weeks, may dispose
of their property at their pleasure, and leave the
soil of this government.'" Although this was in
direct violation and contravention of the charter
of the Town, which assured them the right of
choosing their local civil officers, and the fullest
liberty of conscience, the resolute Governor did
not hesitate or pause in his course.

May 17th, 1563, Governor Stuyvesant put forth
a still more severe edict, proclaiming vengence

and heavy penalties upon skippers and barques that should smuggle into the colony any of those "abominable impostors, runaways, and strolling people called Quakers."

In 1664 followed the transfer to England, which closed the Governor's official relation with the colony.

Yet the Quakers were not exempt from annoyances and vexations as appears from the following:

"The sentence of William Bishop of fflushing, for uttering seditious words.

"The Governor being informed that one Wm. Bishop had spoken seditious words at a publique meeting of ye Inhabitants of the Towne of Fflushing, before his Honor, on ye 3d of this instant month.

"Captain Richard Betts declareth that at the time and place aforementioned, after the Governor, among other matters, had told the people then met together, that he would furnish them with powder for their present occasions and would be content to receive fire-wood for it: he heard Wm. Bishop speak those words aloud, (vizt.) 'That there was another cunning trick.' Upon which the said Capt. Betts told ye said Bishop that if he had any thing to say in answer to what had been proposed by the Governor, he was best to speak it to the Governor himselfe who was

hard by, and not to mutter such words among
the people—to which he made answer : ' It is
very like that he hath sett ye here to hearken to
what we say, that you may tell him.'  Whereunto Capt. Betts replied, ' It was not so, but since
he thought so, he should take further notice of
what he said.'  Then Bishop returned answer,
' What have I said ?  I said nothing, but there
is another cunning trick.'  Dated at New York
July 8th, 1667.

" The contents of what is within wrytten being
read and attested in the presence of Wm. Bishop,
it was likewise by him confest before the Governor.

" July 9th, 1667.  For seditious words spoken
at Fflushing upon the 3d of July, by William
Bishop, the said William Bishop is sentenced to
be made fast to the whipping-post, there to stand
with rodds fastened to his back during the sitting
of the Court of Mayor and Aldermen, and from
thence to be conveyed unto the *Comon Goale* till
further order.  By order of Governor and Council·
MATTHIAS NICHOLS, *Secretary*."

" Oct. 3d, 1701.  To the Honorable John Nan-
fan, Esq., Governor and Commander in Chief of
the Province of New York, &c. :

" The humble petition of Samuel Haight, John
Way and Robert Field on behalf of themselves
5

and the rest of the ffreeholders of Queens County, of the persuasion and profession of the people called Quakers.

"*Sheweth*, Unto yo[r] Honour that lately in the eleccon of Representatives to assist in Generall Assembly, in Queens County, the petitioners abovenamed, and others of their profession, have been interrupted and deprived of their right and privilege of voting by the Justices of s[d] County, or some of them, and others appointed witnesses to the eleccon, upon pretence and color of not having taken the oaths notwithstanding their having signed the declaracon, appointed the people of that persuasion by act of Parliament.

"There being another eleccon to be had in said County in a few days that the peticoners may enjoy their rights and privileges and to prevent controversy for the future :

"They therefore humbly pray to have yor honours opinion whether they, being qualified otherways to vote for representatives in such eleccons are legally barrd and precluded from doing thereof by their not swearing, and as in duty bound, &c.

SAMUEL HAIGHT,
JOHN WAY,
ROBERT FFIELD."

The following list shows the amount of money

taken from the Quakers of the town of Flushing, Dec. 1st, 1756.

| | | | |
|---|---|---|---|
| John Thorn, | £2 | James Persons, | £2 |
| James Burling, | 2 | Danll Lathum, | 2 |
| James Bowne | 2 | Samuel Thorne, | 2 |
| Benj. Doughty, | 2 | Caleb Field, | 2 |
| Stephen Hedger, | 2 | John Thorne, | 1 |
| Danl. Bowne, | 2 | | —— |
| | | | £21 |

This was done under cover of law, " Pursuant to two Acts of General Assembly of the Province of New York"

In instructions to Gov. Dongan is the following article :

" You shall permit all persons of what religion soever, quietly to inhabit within yo$^r$ Government without giving them any disturbance or disquiet whatsoever, for or by reason of their differing opinions in matters of Religion, Provided they give noe disturbance to ye publick peace, nor doe molest or disquiet others in ye free exercise of their Religion. 29th day of May, 1686."

The only connection of this with our history is, that the inhabitants of Flushing were affected by it, equally with other portions of the province, and were entitled to the freedom in religious matters it enjoins upon the Governor.

*Earl of Bellmont to the Lords of trade.*

"Upon reading a bill" (to the Assembly) "where were the words (late happy revolution,) Captain Whitehead moved that the word (happy) might be left out, for he said he did not conceive the revolution to be happy. Captain Whitehead is one of the members that serves for Queen's County, on Nassau Island; he keeps a publick house at a town called Jamaica, and is a disciple of Nicholl's. 'Tis at his house that Nicholls had always a rendevouz with his pirates in Colonel Fletcher's time, and twice the last summer as I afterwards heard, and which was sworn to by John Williamson, whose deposition I sent your Lordships with my packet of the 21st of last October. Nicholls has so poysoned the people of Queen's County, who are all English, that $\frac{2}{3}$ parts of them are said to be down right Jacobites, and to avoid taking the oaths to the King, which I lately injoined all the males in the Province to do from 16 years old and upwards—a great many men in that Country pretend themselves Quakers to avoid taking the oaths; but soon after at the election of Assembley-men those very men pulled off the mask of Quakerism and were got very drunk and swore and fought bloodily; their patrone Mr. Nicholls being a spectator all the while.

New York, Aprill the 27th, 1699,"

The following is part of a "Petition of the Protestants of New York to King William III."

"Citty of New York 30th December, 1701." After the usual preliminaries it continues :

"Wee your Majesties Protestant subjects in your Plantation of New York in America, having too many reiterated Informations of our being calumniated and misrepresented to your Majesty, with hearts full of grief, Loyalty, and the highest duty and regard to your Majesty humbly pray the Freedom to acquaint your Majesty." It then proceeds to enumerate their grievances, " great partiality in appointment of officers, Manifest corruption and injustice in all Elections, &c. &c."

" Wee underwritten in behalf of ourselves and about two thirds of the freeholders and inhabitants of Queens County on Nassau Island.

Tho. Willett,　　　　Tho. Hicx,
Daniel Whitehead,　Jonathan Smith,
　　　　John Taalman."

" Nov. 17th, 1759. A Great celebration was held at Flushing over the reduction of Quebec, that long dreaded sink of French perfidy and cruelty. An elegant and sumptuous entertainment was served, at which the principal inhabitants of the Town were present. Toasts, celebrating the paternal tenderness of our Most gracious Sover-

5*

eign—the patriotism and integrity of Mr. Pitt—
the fortitude and activity of the Generals, &c.
were drunk with all the honors. Every toast was
accompanied by discharge of Cannon, which
amounted to over 100. In the evening a large
bon fire and splendid illumination.

Cadwallader Colden, while holding the office of
Lieutenant Governor, built a spacious and sub
stantial mansion on the property now owned by
John H. Brower, Esq., which was then called
" Spring Hill." Here the Gov. died Sept. 20th,
1776. He was buried in a private cemetery attached to the farm. We have carefully examined
this burial-plot, but can find no record to indicate "the narrow house" where his mortal remains sleep, awaiting the awakening, the last
day. The only records decipherable are those of
deaths in the Willett family. Of these there are
but few. We give one :

> " *Here lies enterred the body of Sarah wife*
> *of Rob. Whiting and daughter of Charles*
> *and Ellena Willett who departed this*
> *life the 7th July 1797 aged 88 years.*
> *Also Willett her Son who departed this*
> *life the 12th April 1792 aged 6 years.*"??*

David Colden, the son of Gov. Colden inherit-

---

* If these figures be correct it involves a physiological problem which
the author leaves to the Committee for solution

ed the estate. He was an ardent and active loyalist in the Revolution. The property was therefore confiscated and sold by forfeiture—being purchased by Walter Burling,* who kept a store where Flushing Hotel now stands. Colden, with his wife Ann, daughter of John Willett, of Flushing, retired to England, where he died July 10th, 1784, and she in August, 1785. Their son, Cadwallader D. Colden, who was born at Spring Hill, April 4th, 1769, returned to this country and became very eminent as a lawyer, legislator and author—being the associate of Hamilton, Livingston and De Witt Clinton. He died at Jersey City, Feb'y 7th, 1834.

Gov. George Clinton also had his residence somewhere in our Town, exactly where, we have not been able to discover. We find only the following notice of his residence in this place:

"Journal of Conrad Weiser's visit to the Mohocks Country. Aug. 27th, 1753—I went to Flushing, on Long Island, seventeen Miles from New York. to wait on Governor Clinton—he happened to be from home but came in by one o'clock. I paid him my Compliments at his Door—he called me in and asked me how far I had been, and signified to me that it was a wrong step in me to proceed to Albany before I had his Directions. I asked Par-

* A son of Walter Burling died at Flushing January 18th, 1859' in the 90th year of his age.

don and told him my Reason why I proceeded. His Excellency said it was well, he did not disapprove so much of my Proceeding as of my Son's not staying for an Answer. His Excellency seemed well enough pleased with my Return, and of my not proceeding to Onondago, and was pleased to tell me that he intended to be in New York next Wednesday, and would then have me to wait on him and take a Letter to Governor Hamilton, and so dismissed me, but would have me stay and eat a Bit of Victuals first, and ordered his Attendance accordingly to get it for me and my Companion. After Dinner I left Flushing and arrived in New York the same Evening

Aug. 29th—His Excellency arrived in New York in the Evening."

The manufacturing of clay tobacco pipes and other articles was carried on to some extent. A number of notices, advertisements, &c. are yet to be seen. We give the following, viz:

" March 31, 1735—6. The Widow of Thomas Parington offers for Sale her farm at Whitestone opposite Frog's point. It has 20 acres of clay ground fit for making tobacco-pipes."

" May 13, 1751. Any person desirous may be supplied with vases, urns, flowerpots, &c. to adorn gardens and tops of houses, or any other ornament made of Clay by Edmond Aunely at

Whitestone—he having sot up the potter's business by means of a German family that he bought, who are supposed by their work to be the most ingenious that ever arrived in America. He has Clay capable of making eight different kinds of ware."

There were patriots in those early days, even as now, willing to serve their country, as appears from the following election card, ninety-five years ago :—

"John Willett, Esq., of Flushing, through the earnest persuasion of his friends, and his desire to serve his country, offers himself as Candidate at the ensuing election of Representatives from Queen's County, which is to be held at Jamaica, on the 23d of May, 1764."

The following letter is a beautiful testimony to a noble act, performed by our ancestors, for the army engaged in fighting with the Indians :

" *To the Representatives of Queen's County.*
Octob. 10, 1755.
Gentlemen,

A few days ago I received a letter from Messrs Schuyler & Depeister, of Albany acquainting me that you had sent to them 69 cheeses and 200 sheep, being part of 1000 raised in Queen's County on Long Island as a present to this Army, and which they had forwarded to me. This letter was read at a Council of War, consisting of all the field officers in this Camp, which I summoned yesterday afternoon.

The most equitable and useful division hath been made of this generous and public-spirited present, which we could follow.

The Cattle and a few sheep had been sent by some of the Provinces to their Troops, yet your sheep were very Seasonable, and highly beneficial to the Army in general. Your cheeses were highly acceptable and reviving; for unless amongst some of the Officers, it was food Scarcely Known among us.

This generous humanity of Queen's County is unanimously and gratefully applauded by all here; we pray that your benevolence may be returned to you by the Great Shepherd of human Kind, a hundred fold; and may those Amiable housewives, to whose skill we owe the refreshing cheeses, long continue to shine in their useful and endearing stations.

I beg, Gentlemen, that you in particular will accept of, and convey to your generous county, my grateful & respectful salutations for their seasonable beneficence to the Army under my command.     I am Gentlemen,

Your Most obedient and Obliged Servant,

W. Johnson."

It is very interesting in reading the reports of the Governors to the authorities in the mother country, to watch how the spark of resistance to their exactions gradually increased in intenseness and volume, until it burst forth in the unconquerable fire of the revolution. Some of these had sagacity and penetration to foresee the utter impracticability of these attempts, and to foretell the consequences of persistance in them. Gov. Tyron, in writing to the Earl of Dartmouth, from " New York, 4th July, 1773," says :

" If it were the wish it is not in the power of any one Province to accommodate with Great Britain, being overawed and controuled by the General confederacy. *Oceans of blood may be spilt* but in my opinion America will *never* receive parliamentary Taxation." This brings us to the subject of the next chapter.

# CHAPTER III.

## REVOLUTIONARY AND OTHER INCIDENTS.

The American Revolution! At its mention, what intense emotions of national pride, and of grateful thanksgiving to the "God of Nations," thrill the heart of patriotism, beating strong in the bosom of every son and daughter of America, worthy of their noble birth-right. It was our national heroic era; the age of heroic men, leagued in a heroic struggle for freedom from colonial servitude and oppression; its glorious record is crystallized in words and deeds, exhibiting a pure, exalted heroism in their intrinsic excellence, and in the vast, incalculable influences, thence resulting and spreading over our whole national history. "Its strong remembrance becomes a part of the national life." It throbs with every pulsation of the national heart. It courses through every vein and artery of the national system, imparting a peculiar complexion to national appearances—a peculiar tinge to national emotions and constituting the entire national creature a very different being from what it would otherwise have been. Its bright and glorious reminiscences are treasured as precious beyond calculation.

The halo, encircling the names of its mighty men, and its consecrated places, made sacred by bloody baptisms, becomes more beauteous and glowing as the chariot of time rolls onward in its rapid march ; " the dust of centuries" will but brighten its resplendent glow.

Hence every incident connected with the war for maintaining the immortal " Declaration of Independence," is dear to the lover of his country. We have none of startling interest connected with our town to communicate. More doubtless might have been collected a few years since, but are now consigned to oblivion with the passing away from earth of those in whose memories was their only record. We must therefore be content with such as we have been able to gather.

Hessian troops to the number of eight or ten thousand were quartered for a considerable period on this part of Long Island, extending from Jamaica to Whitestone. The first detachment came from Jamaica. As the cavalry were coming down what is now Jamaica avenue, some boys were indulging their curiosity in looking at them. Becoming frightened they took refuge in a barn which stood a few rods north of Sandford Hall. Looking out from their hiding place they saw a portion detach themselves from the main-body. They came to the barn and called upon the rebels to come forth and surrender, or they would fire the building. The boys, thinking they would carry their threat into execution, came out in very great trepidation, supposing, doubtless, they were to be at once made prisoners. The soldiers, seeing they were *only boys*, rode back to their comrades, to the great relief of the young patriots.

We have not been able to fix the locality of the several encampments. One was at Fresh Meadows, close by the present residence of Jacob Duryea; another was along the Manhasset road, near a piece of woods just beyond the residence of John Bowne. Their object of course was to protect the several roads and highways, as this section was very important in a strategical point of view, in consequence of the narrowness of the river opposite Whitestone.

The troops were billetted at different farm houses. Their principal quarters were the old Bowne house on Bowne avenue, the old stone house just beyond Flushing cemetery, now occupied by Whitehead Duryea, and the house on Whitestone avenue, now the residence of Watson Bowron. The Aspinwall house (now Joseph T. Darling's) was the head quarters for the officers. A sentinel was constantly stationed in front of this house. The inhabitants of the place were accustomed to ride much on horse-back; but

FRIENDS MEETING HOUSE.

(BICKSITE)

in passing this retreat of these mighty men of valor and honor, they were compelled to dismount and perform this part of their journey on foot.

The old meeting house of the Friends was occupied as a prison, hospital and hay-magazine. "When the British officer first went to take possession Friends were in silent meeting. He put his head in the door, but seeing them sit so quiet and demure, he withdrew till shaking hands was over"—a fact creditable, we think, both to him and to them—and reminding one of Lamb's Essay on a "Quaker Meeting"—in which he says "here is something which throws antiquity herself in the foreground—Silence—eldest of things—language of Old Night—primitive discourser—to which the insolent decays of mouldering grandeur have but arrived by a violent, and as we may say, unnatural progression.

> How reverned is the view of those hushed heads,
> Looking tranquility;

and from which, he says, "you go away with a sermon not made with hands."

A Col. Hamilton was at one time in command of the troops stationed here. His head quarters were in the house now owned and occupied by Wm. Mitchell. Being of an overbearing, domineering disposition, tradition reports that he required every person who met him to salute his

Highness with a very deferential bow. If his demand was not complied with, he stormed terribly.

Their cannon were placed upon the high ground, fronting the residence of S. B. Parsons; and to the great terror of all young urchins of color in the neighborhood, the artillery daily practised to perfect themselves in the art of shooting the rebels.

While the troops were occupying the old stone house, a neighbor missed a pig. The Hessians were suspected of stealing it, but no positive proof could be obtained. Upon closer inspection, however, it was tracked by the blood to this house, up stairs, and found in a bed; and with it was a a companion. The dead pig, and a live Hessian were bed-fellows; or according to another tradition, which we are unwilling to credit, a woman was covered with the same blankets as the pig!

The property owned by the late Col. Benj. R. Hoagland was also occupied by a body of troops. They made their quarters in the barn. An elderly lady, still living, Miss Catharine Hoagland, remembers the fact, that a little child belonging to one of the soldiers died, and that she went to the barn to look at the corpse.

The soldiers were much given to plunder; and especially the cattle of the farmers were objects of covetous desire and forcible seizure. James Bowne, grand-father of our fellow townsman,

Walter Bowne, who lived where Thomas S. Willetts now resides, was awakened in the night by a disturbance in his barn yard. Hoisting the window and exposing the upper part of his body that he might discover what was the difficulty, one of the villains discharged a musket at him. The ball took effect in the arm, inflicting a severe wound. His son Walter, father of the present Walter, a lad about ten years old, passed through the British camp in the neighborhood, and went some distance through the woods, at 12 o'clock at night, to the house of his uncle Willett Bowne, where John Bowne now resides, and told what had happened. He and his cousin William, a lad about the same age, father of John, Scott H. and Benj. Bowne, and grandfather of Stephen and Cornell Bowne, at Ireland Mills, then went over to what is now the *farm* house of Walter Bowne, opposite the residence of Simon Bowne, for Dr. Belden. He at once came and rendered the necessary surgical service. The old gentleman thus saved his cattle, but at the expense of a musket ball in his arm.

Willett Bowne was also subjected to the trials of the "times that tried men's souls." Some parties, blackened and disguised in various ways, entered his house one night and demanded his cash. This he refused to part with so uncere-

6*

moniously and without an equivalent. They then tied his hands to the bed-post and applied a lighted candle to the ends of his fingers in the hope that under the potency and virtue of *fiery* arguments he would be induced to disclose the hiding place of his treasures. But these were more precious to him than the tips of his fingers, and with resolute fortitude he refused to "deliver." After torturing him till they were satisfied it was useless, they left him with sore fingers, a light heart, but with a heavy purse. The old gentleman recognized the persons, notwithstanding their disguise, but to the day of his death refused to prosecute them, or tell who they were—thus exhibiting a noble magnanimity that justly entitles him to honorable mention among the many worthies of those perilous times.

The women of Flushing also suffered indignities and ruffianism at the hands of the troops. These hirelings of despotism, would enter, at any hour of the night, any house, in which it was known there were none but women—compel them to get up and prepare supper for them—requiring the best things the house afforded. At the house of Joseph Wright, in Whitestone, there were assembled, for greater security, the females of two families—the men being away from home. Looking out of the window, they saw five or six horsemen coming toward the house, leaping over the fences. " You are a fine parcel of women" says one " where is the man of the house?" " He is out in the field," " Well, did he take fire-arms with him?" " No, he is an old man, too old to use fire-arms." They then turned and left, doing no other harm than causing something of a fright.

Although we have not been able to gather individual instances, we doubt not the women of Flushing displayed a heroism equal to any emergency. It was the noble heart of true woman, that in ancient times led a mother to say to her son, as she handed him his shield, " bring this back, or be brought back upon it." It was the noble heart of noble woman, that, in the late great rebellion in India, nerved the wife of one to grasp the reins and whip and lash the foaming steeds through ranks of savage Sepoys, while her husband plied his revolver and musket; and spurring on till another gang was reached, who had stretched a a rope across the road, yet faltered not, but still urged on the steeds, and though they stumbled, yet by aid of whip and rein, she kept them on, and her husband still with sword and gun smiting down the wretches who endeavored to climb into their carrriage. And so both escaped with their lives, but not without wounds. *Such is Woman.*

Prince William, afterward William IV, predecessor of Queen Victoria—visited Flushing, while in this country. A grand jubilee was held, and an ox was roasted in honor of the event.

Gen. Washington also visited Flushing, being the guest of Wm. Prince, grandfather of Wm. R· Prince, our fellow citizen. This was short!y after the Revolutionary War. James Rantas, an aged colored man still living in the village says he remembers this fact distinctly. A large tent made of cedar bushes and other evergreens was erected and extended diagonally from Alfred C. Smith's corner toward the Flushing Hotel. In this were tables abundantly spread, and dinner was served. When the people were shouting and swinging their hats, Washington, who wore a three cornered hat, raised his and bowed in recognition of their approbation.

There is, or was, until lately, a redoubt on the property of John Haggerty, at Whitestone. Tradition says, this was thrown up by order and under the supervision of Gen. Washington.

"Oct. 6, 1779, Oliver Thorne was master of the Flushing freight and passenger boat, which lies near the ferry stairs, N. Y."

"Dec. 11, 1790, Mr. Gilbert Seasman of Flushing fell overboard of Capt. Thos. H. Smith's passage boat, a little above Hell Gate, and was drowned.

It would appear that one of the first Railroads ever put in operation, was the one now familiarly known as "the underground Railroad."

Witness the following :—

"Nov. 27, 80. . To be sold, a healthy negro man and woman, neither in the least infatuated with a desire of obtaining freedom by flight, which so unhappily reigns throughout the generality of negroes at present.

DAVID COLDEN, Esq. Flushing."

Here we have the following dubious advertisement :—

"May 21, '81. J. Holroyd thanks the gentlemen of the Army and Navy, and informs them that he has *opened* the QUEEN'S HEAD at Flushing.' How he came into possession of the royal *Caput* is not stated ; nor whether he was *capitally* punished for the murderous deed.

In 1791, John Bowne and Nathaniel Persall were elected members to the Legislature, from Queen's County. They were Friends and refused to take "the oaths directed by the Governor's Commission." They were accordingly dismissed, and their seats declared vacant.

Aug. 4, 1825, Judge Lawrence of Bay Side gave $340 for one Saxony Sheep. For a considerable period the merino-sheep fever raged furiously in this section of the country, and the inhabitants of Flushing did not escape the contagion. There is still extant a letter from Wm. S. Burling to Samuel Parsons, dated New York, 8th mo. 31st, 1810; from which I make an extract or two, bearing upon the subject. After inviting him to come and see the two sheep he had purchased, he says, " they are pronounced by the best judges to be equal to any they have seen. From the sample of wool I have seen, I am persuaded they are as fine as the Buck lately bo't by Effingham Lawrence, T. Buckley & Co. and far superior to Whitehead, Hicks & Co. I should be unwilling to give my two for their three. But that thou may judge for thyself, I send thee a small sample of wool taken from the shoulder of each." The samples are still attached to the letter. So very minute are they, that they could be easily compressed into a child's thimble. I suppose the considerate Friend feared to take away much, lest the exposure should prove fatal to his pets ; or having many acquaintances to whom to send samples, but little could be spared for each. After some further history of them he says, "I had the choice of fifty-two, and I have no reason to believe they are exceeded by any in this State. I have no doubt that I could readily get $2,250 for them, but I have no idea of selling either. They appear to be in good health and are thriving nicely."

We are told that almost forty years since, sabbath desecration was exceedingly prevalent, and especially among the colored people. They would also congregate at night in different places around the village: Forming a circle, with a fiddler or some one to sing, they would dance and shout, to the great discomfort of the more quiet and orderly portion of the community. Their drunken brawls and fights in the streets were a nuisance to all. Some of the citizens determined to secure the peace by arresting one and another and having them fined or committed to jail. But they failed. The young men, mostly apprentices, then took the matter in hand, and formed themselves into an association, called by the euphonious and suggestive name of "the Rotten Egg Society." They collected all the spoiled eggs they could obtain ; and concealing themselves at a little distance, discharged battery after battery into the midst of the sable brawlers. This proved more potent than " the strong arm of the Law." Fancy the consternation and confusion amid the colored ranks, as these tremendous missiles came pouring in upon them from invisible foes !

In 1841, when Linnæus St. was opened, a dozen or more human skeletons were thrown up in grading. Leaden bullets were found with them. This would indicate that these once animate forms had fallen in battle, probably in some revolutionary conflict. Skeletons were also found on the Redwood property, in excavating some years since.

# CHAPTER IV.

COMMUNICATION WITH THE CITY—SLOOPS—STEAM-
BOATS—RAIL ROADS—POST OFFICE—APPEARANCE
OF THE VILLAGE—FIRE AND MILLITARY COMPA-
NIES—OTHER ASSOCIATIONS, &C.—WHITESTONE—
COLLEGE POINT—LITTLE NECK.

In former times the route to New York was by
the Head of the Fly, or Vleigh, the Dutch word for
meadow, through Jamaica and Bedford to Brooklyn,
a distance of from seventeen to twenty miles. To
obviate this, Wm. Prince, the second of that name,*
organized a company of which he was chosen President, with a capital of $12,500, of which $10,000
was raised. This company procured a charter for
the erection of the bridge over Flushing Creek.
This bridge was built in 1800, was washed away in
1802, was rebuilt, and has since been rebuilt sev-

---

* John Prince came from England to Boston somewhere between the
years 1660—70. He had two sons who came to Long Island, and settled
at Flushing. The family name, on the elder brother's side, is extinct·
He had *one* son, that son had *thirteen* daughters, but not one son. The
younger brother, Albert, was grandfather of Wm. Prince, the first
nurseryman in Flushing. *His* son, Wm. is the one above referred to ·
His son is Wm. R Prince, our fellow townsman. Wm. Prince the 2d
was of an enterprising, amiable and kindly character, universally es-
teemed in life, and regretted in death.

7

eral times. This considerably shortened the route to New York. Shortly after, through the exertions of Wm. Prince, Joshua Sands of Brooklyn, and others, the bridge across the Wallabout was built, still more shortening the route, and giving a new impetus to the growth of the village.

Mr. Prince was also very active in getting up the Flushing and Newtown turnpike. This met with great opposition, especially, it is said, from the Dutch residents along the road. His son tells me he has heard his father say, he found but one favorable to the proposal, and his reason was "that he would like to sit on his stoop and see the people drive past his house." To overcome this opposition, he travelled more than a thousand miles. In all his efforts he was zealously seconded by John Aspinwall, and also by other residents of the village.

Previous to the erection of the bridge persons were conveyed across the creek in small boats. To reach them a kind of path was made with boards down the sides of the meadow. James Rantas and Thomas Smith, two colored men, still living, were for many years ferry-masters. They made no regular charge for ferriage, but left their compensation to the liberality of each passenger. This liberality showed itself in sums varying from one to four cents, very seldom reaching six, and twelve and a-half would have been considered quite a fortune.

*Stage Routes.*—The first effort to run a stage between Flushing and New York was in 1801. The route was through Newtown and Bedford to Brooklyn—Fare 50 cents, Willett Mott, proprietor. He continued for seven years, and was followed by Carman Smith, Greenwall and Kissam. John Boyd, who drove for seventeen years, and was the first who ran to Williamsburg, across Grand st. ferry, up Grand to Bowery, and down to Chatham Square—Fare 56 cents; and since then a number of proprietors, for short periods, until four years ago, the route was abandoned. The stages were exchanged for the locomotive.

*Steam Boats.*—The first water communication with the city was, as we have said, by a large Indian canoe. This was succeeded by sloops running more or less frequently, as circumstances required. Their landing place in Flushing, previous to 1800, was at the slip and dock where Peck & Fairweather now have their coal yard  After the erection of the bridge the present town dock was built for their accommodation. Howell Smith owned and ran a packet, as it was termed. He was succeeded by Samuel Pryor, with the same vessel. He was bought out by Jonathan R.

Peck, father of Isaac Peck, who built a new
vessel with ample and more elegant accommodations. He was followed by his eldest son, Jonathan, who ran daily, regulating by the state of the
tide, his hours for leaving and returning.

A small steam boat ran for a season as an experiment about 1822. But the first that ran regularly was built expressly for this route, and commenced her trips in 1823. She was named Linnæus,
and was commanded by Capt. Jonathan Peck.
She was a very superior boat for those times. She
ran here about ten years, and was then transferred
to run between New York and New Rochelle.
She was followed by

the Flushing, Capt. Curtis Peck,
Then came the Statesman, " Elijah Peck,
" Star, " " "
" Washington Irving, " Stephen Leonard,
" Island City, " Silas Reynolds,
" Enoch Dean, " Wm. Reynolds.
The channel in Flushing Bay was dredged and
deepened for the first time in 1833; the second in
1857, and last in 1859.

In 1859 the Flushing, College Point and New
York Steam Ferry Company was organized.
They now run the steamer Enoch Dean, but before this leaves the press the Company expect to
have running, in connection with it, a new Iron

Steam Boat, costing about $40,000--the first Iron Boat ever run on the East River. This is a movement in the right direction, bearing directly upon the prosperity of the village.

*Rail Road.*—This was built, and commenced operation in 1854. Its fortunes have not been very favorable to stockholders. It was first sold to the bondholders; then, in 1859, to Oliver Charlick, of New York, and by him in 1860, to E. B. Litchfield. Since its construction the village has grown rapidly to the southward in the neighborhood of its terminus. Our inhabitants have frequent daily communication with the city. With these and the other inducements our village offers, as a desirable place of residence, especially for business men in the city, its rapid growth would seem to be beyond a peradventure.

*Post Office.*—The first Post Office in the town was located at the Alley, where was a woollen manufactory,* which was burned down a few years since. It was removed to the village about 1822. There was considerable opposition to the change, even by many of the villagers. One principal reason for opposing it was, it is said,

---

* Some other factories have been in operation in the town, but we have not been able to obtain much information about them.

7*

that their letters and papers were now left at the Hotel where they could get them at any time, which they could not do, if the office was kept at the village and only open at certain hours. This reason probably weighed all the more powerfully as they were thus afforded a good excuse to visit the Hotel for something not carried in Uncle Sam's mail bags.

The *first* Post Master in the village was Curtis Peck, who kept the office in the Pavillion.

The *second* was his brother Wm. Peck, who kept a store on the site now occupied by Peck & Fairweather.

The *third* was the late Dr. Joseph Bloodgood, who held the office for sixteen years.

The *fourth* was Dr. Asa Spalding, who held the office about four years, and during part of this time there were two mails a day.

The *fifth* was the late Francis Bloodgood, who held the office for ten years, in the store of Clement & Bloodgood.

The *sixth* and present incumbent, Charles W. Cox, was appointed in 1854.

*Appearance of the Town, Village, &c.*—The surface of the town is moderately undulating. The soil is of very superior quality, and is in a high state of cultivation. Agriculture "pays" with the farmers of Flushing. There are very many charming sites for genteel residences, and these are rapidly being taken up and occupied by gentlemen of leisure, or of business from the city, who prefer for their families and for themselves after their day's toils, the quiet comforts and enjoyments, and the health-imparting air, of a home in the country.

About sixty years ago there were only from forty to fifty houses in the village. Where are now Bowne Avenue, Ailanthus Place, Amity, Union, Washington, Liberty, Madison, Cottage Row, Church, Locust, Cedar, Orange and Prince streets, thickly studded with residences and stores, there was only here and there a dwelling. It is not more than twenty years since a large orchard occupied the grounds through which now run Madison street and Cottage Row. At that time the erection of a new house created quite an excitement, and people wondered whereunto it would grow. Then too there was no dock where the town dock now is; and all around where the lumber and coal yards now are, were low marshy grounds.

Where the Town Hall now stands, and the surrounding grounds, formerly was a sylvan lake, embowered in overarching trees with their beauteous foliage, and emitting an ambrosial fragrance which the classic poets might have consecrated to their Deities——*the village pond* about seventy-five feet wide and two hundred feet long. In reference to this, one* of the Presidents of the Board of Trustees remarks :—" too filthy for frogs or fish, and only valuable for the amusement it afforded the skaters during winter, and during summer for the cattle to cool themselves and slake their thirst." But its glory is departed. " Sic transit gloria mundi."

Just east of the pond, and in front of the old Friends' meeting-house, " arose a perpendicular bank some eight feet high, where the school-boy amused himself by leaping into the sand below."

*Bridge street* was then *so narrow* as but just to admit the passage of two vehicles.

The grade of Main Street, in front of the Episcopal church was on a level with the *top rail* of the fence in front of Mr. Garretson's dwelling opposite the church.

None of the streets were flagged. Bridge street was paved in 1853.

*Incorporation of Village.*—The Charter of Incorporation of the village of Flushing bears date April 15th, 1837. The first meeting of the Board of Trustees was held June 6th, 1837. The first President of the Board was Robert B. Van Zandt.

---

* Hon. John W. Lawrence.

THE FIRST CONGREGATIONAL CHURCH.

The Charter has since been amended and the incorporated limits somewhat extended. Its present boundaries are, " All that certain tract of land in the town of Flushing, county of Queens, embraced within the following bounds that is to say : Commencing at a point in the east side of Whitestone avenue, three hundred feet north of Bayside avenue ; thence north eighty-four degrees forty-five minutes east, seven hundred and fifty-six feet ; thence south four degrees twenty-five minutes east, two thousand four hundred and ninety-six feet to the south side of the street called Broadway ; thence south fourteen degrees east, three thousand five hundred and forty-four feet to a point in land of William Smart ; thence south fifty-nine degrees twenty-five minutes west, two thousand six hundred and forty-nine feet to and along the Ireland avenue to a point near the small creek ; thence north eighty-three degrees ten minutes west, three thousand nine hundred and sixty-one feet to Flushing creek ; thence along the same about five thousand three hundred feet in a northerly course to the Flushing Mill Pond ; thence along the same Mill Pond about two thousand two hundred feet to or near another small stream ; thence south eighty-four degrees forty-eight minutes east, two thousand four hundred and fifty feet to the place of beginning.—

shall continue to be known and distinguished as the VILLAGE OF FLUSHING."

The Trustees of the Village for 1860, are John W. Lawrence, John S. Pittman, Charles Miller, Alexander Parks, Joseph Harris King and Henry Clement.

In 1837 the number of real-estate holders was one hundred and three ; in 1857 there were over four hundred.

The assessed value of taxable property was
in 1837,..............................$465,300
in 1857, ..............$1,325,350

Increase in 20 years, $860,050

This growth and the various improvements have not been reached without commendable public spirit and enterprise. In the first *seven* years there were expended upon the public streets, for grading, paving, &c., $30,000. Of this $1,000 only could be raised annually by taxation; $50 of which was paid to the collector, leaving an aggregate of $6,650. The balance of $23,350 was wholly raised by voluntary contributions.

The present village Hall was built in 1843, at a cost of $1,009. Previous to this the Board held its meetings generally in the houses of its members.

Some idea of the business of the village, at

present, may be formed from the schedule from the Flushing Journal of January 1st, 1859, to be found in the appendix.

To this we shall add a brief statement of some other matters.

Owing to frequent robberies a night watch was established by private subscription in 1855.

*Sand Paper Factory.*—This was built in 1851, by W. B. Parsons & Co., for the manufacture of Sand, Emery and Match paper. It formerly employed fifty hands; now, in consequence of improved machinery, employs ten. Present firm, Joseph T. More & Co.

*Gas Company*—This was incorporated Oct. 6th, 1855, with a capital stock of $20,000; and the exclusive right of supplying the village with gas for twenty years. The length of the street mains laid is two and a-half miles. The quantity of gas made per month will average 100,000 cubic feet. The number of street lamps erected is eighteen. The company had fifty meters at the commencement; now they have more than double that number. The Stockholders are

James R. Lowerre, *President*,

Gilbert Hicks, *Treasurer*,

Charles A. Willets, *Secretary*.

*Steam Planing and Saw Mill.*—J. Milnor Peck, proprietor. The first mill was built June 13th, 1851.

It was a frame building, three stories high. The second and third stories were occupied by Messrs. Cox & Dumont for sash-making. In the first story, beside the planing and sawing, Messrs J. C. Quarterman and A. Lewis had turning lathes. The engine was the first stationary steam engine in the place, and was purchased at the Novelty Works, New York.

This building was destroyed by fire Nov. 21, 1853.

June 8th, 1854, the present one story fire-proof building was erected with entire new machinery, for planing, sawing and moulding.

In June, 1856, the three story, brick, fire-proof building adjoining was built. Employs from fourteen to twenty hands.

A Turning and Scroll-Sawing Mill, with engine attached, was built by John H. Quarterman, in 1854. Since his death it is carried on by Geo. A. Stillwagon.

*Fire Companies.*—One or two efforts were early made to sustain the fire companies in the village. Forty years ago a company was organized—one Stansbury was Captain. He was succeeded by Capt. Treadwell Sands, who had charge for twenty years; but it was not until April, 1854, that the present Fire Department was organized. William Post, Chief Engineer; Henry S. Hover and E. P. Van

Velsor, Assistants. It embraces four companies; Mutual Fire Engine Co. No. 1; Young America, No. 2; Excelsior Hook and Ladder, and Empire Hose. The department is well equiped and efficiently manned. There are also several public cisterns or reservoirs of water for the extinguishment of fires. The whole cost of the Fire Department, including buildings, is about $12,000.

Of No. 1, E. P. Creasy was first foreman, succeeded by C. W. Cox; of No. 2, Adam S. Penfold was first foreman, succeeded by Joseph P. Stillwagon; Hook and Ladder Co., Geo. A. Stillwagon was first foreman, succeeded by Geo. H. Quarterman, who was again succeeded by Geo. A. Stillwagon; of Hose Co., Oscar W. Smith is foreman.

*Military.*—The Flushing Guard, the first uniformed military organization in this town, was commissioned Nov. 1st, 1839, as Light Infantry. It was attached to the 93d Regiment, N. Y. S. M. as a flank company. It made its first parade with twenty-six uniforms, Jan. 16th, 1840. It attained a high state of discipline. In Feb. 1843 its designation was changed to Artillery. In June, 1845 it was again changed to Light Horse Artillery, and attached to Storm's famous 1st Brigade, L. H. A., in which it excelled. Its brilliant appearance excited the admiration of its old

commander, Major General Jones, who, seeing it
with harnessed battery, careering over the field at
a review, turned to his Brigadier, Heriman, and
exclaimed, "You have lost the flower of your
Brigade." In 1848 it had attained a State-wide
reputation for excellency in the L. H. A. evolu-
tions. Its parades called together the most celebrated tacticians in the army, who styled it "the
incomparable," and gave it the name of "Bragg's
Battery," after the Hero of Buena Vista. At the
breaking out of the Mexican war, its services
were unanimously tendered to government, but
not accepted. After varied fortunes for a period
of twenty years, it still exists in good discipline,
ready when its country needs its services, to again
appear the foremost.

The Flushing Guard was first commanded by
Capt. Charles A. Hamilton; then by Capt. Wm.
A. Mitchell. Since its change to Bragg's Bat-
tery, it has been commanded by Capt. Thomas
L Robinson.

Company A, Hamilton Rifles, was organized
January 24th, 1849. They are the first Battalion
Company in the 15th Regiment, which is com-
manded by Col. Charles A. Hamilton, and com-
prises Queens Co. Its officers, commissioned by
Gov. Fish, are Geo. B. Roe, Captain; Henry A.
Peck, 1st Lieut.; Henry S. Barto, 2d Lieut.

ASSOCIATIONS.

*Rechabites.*—The "Sons of Rechab" were organized for the promotion of total abstinence principles, March 14th, 1845. They surrendered their charter in 1855.

*Sons of Temperance*—Were organized April 14th, 1843. They number forty members, and thirty female visitors, or "Daughters of Temperance."

*The "Pacific Lodge, No. 85, I. O. O. F."*—Was instituted April 19th, 1843. It has had various fortunes. It still continues, however, in efficient working order, numbering fifty members. It has disbursed, for weekly benefits to sick members, an aggregate of $13 50, and for burial expenses $135.

*Young Men's Christian Association.*—This was organized in 1858. It has a good library of religious works for the use of its members : it holds a weekly prayer meeting, and a meeting for literary exercises every two weeks. The members are actively engaged in conducting mission sabbath schools, distributing tracts and attending religious meetings. The association is thus accomplishing much good. May it have a long and prosperous career. Peter Gorsline has been president since its organization.

*Flushing Library Association*—This was organized shortly after the above. Its object is to gather a circulating library of choice books for the use of its members. From its reports it has met thus far, with decided success. The library already numbers 1,100 volumes. Number of members or annual subscribers, in 1860, is 329. May its sun of prosperity continue to shine long.

*The Flushing Debating Society*--Was organized in the autumn of 1859. It numbers twenty-one members, and meets semi-monthly.

The Y. M. C. A., the F. L. A., and the F. D. S. have their rooms over the Drug store of C. H. Hedges, M. D.

*Flushing Harmonic Society.*—Established in 1854. Average number of members twenty-five. The objects of the society are the cultivation of musical taste, and proficiency among its members ; to raise the standard of church music in the various churches in the village ; and to collect a library of valuable musical works for future practice. The meetings for rehearsal are held weekly. The success of the society in attaining the objects sought has been fully attested by their occasional public performances.

*Flushing Reading Association.*—Organized in 1857. The object of this association is to cultivate rhetorical practice by the careful rehearsal of Poetical and Dramatical selections. The number of active members is limited by the constitution to forty. There are also honorary or associate members to the number of twenty. The latter, however, take no part in the exercises, and have no voice in the government of the society. The management is vested solely in a board of three persons, chosen by the association every six weeks, who have entire control of the selection and assignment of parts for reading, who conduct the meetings and manage all the financial concerns of the association. The meetings are held in rotation at the houses of the different members once in two weeks during the winter season.

*The Bay Side Reading Association*—Similar in its object to the one already mentioned—originated in 1858.

*The Flushing Mutual Benevolent Burial Association*—Was organized in 1851, and numbers eighty members. It is composed mainly of Irishmen, who must be citizens of the United States, or have declared their intentions to become such. Its purpose is to create a fund for mutual support when overtaken by infirmities or sickness, and in case of the death of any member, to contribute the necessary means for his decent interment; and in solemn procession to accompany his remains to their last resting place.

*Flushing Sewing Society.*—For the relief of the indigent, held weekly meetings, throughout the

8*

winter season, at the houses of the different members for more than twenty-five years  Originally composed of members of the Episcopal Church only, as the village enlarged, members of other religious denominations became associated with it. During the later period of its existence, with the exception of one or two years, the society met at the hospitable mansion of a lady in the village, who, as President of the association, with true christian benevolence ministered to the wants of the needy, and relieved the necessities of the deserving poor.

*Ladies' Union Aid Society.*—In the winter of 1857—8 the wants of our village poor became so urgent that it was deemed best to make a more general and systematic effort for their relief by the formation of the above mentioned society.  It numbers fifty members, and holds weekly meetings during the winter season in the saloon of the Flushing Institute.

*The Lawrence Boat Club*—Was organized in 1855, and numbers eighteen members.  This Club meets regularly each week, from May to November, for the purpose of rowing.  The club boathouse is on the premises of the Hon. John W. Lawrence, by whom it was donated.

*The Naiad Boat Club*—Was organized in the same year with the preceding.

FLUSHING FEMALE INSTITUTE

*The Queen's Co. Savings Bank*—Obtained its charter from the State Legislature in 1859. The Board of Directors organized in July of the same year, by the election of the Hon. John W. Lawrence, as President, and Walter Bowne, as Vice-President. We feel assured that this new institution will prove a means of great benefit to our community.

*Base Ball Clubs*—Two organizations of this kind exist in our village. It will be seen that our community are alive to the necessity of the cultivation of the physical, as well as the moral and intellectual parts of our nature.

*Flushing Bible Society.*—A branch of the "Long Island Bible Society" was established in 1854. Its first work was to supply every family in our town with a copy of the Holy Scriptures. This was accomplished through the efficient agency of their colporteur. Its efforts were also directed to the establishment of Sunday Schools in parts of our town remote from the village. Since its organization a large number of copies of the Bible and New Testament have been distributed in our midst.

### BURIAL PLACES.

*Private Graveyards.*—Lawrence family, at Bayside; Parsons, at Flushing; Skidmore, at Fresh

Meadows, on the Hoagland farm; Loweree, on the Bowron Farm, Whitestone avenue.

*Church Graveyards.*—These are connected severally with the different churches in the village, viz :—St. George's Church; St. Michael's (R. C.); Friends' meeting house; Methodist Church, at Whitestone, and formerly one was attached to the Methodist Church in Washington street, but was removed in 1857. In the Quaker burial ground nothing was formerly allowed to mark the spot where lay the sleeping dust. A sister, whose husband was laid to rest in that place, was desirous in some way to mark the spot, that it might be identified by her descendants, and she accordingly planted a small walnut tree over his grave. But an old member of the society, staunch in the faith, and zealous in maintaining the integrity of *Foxian* customs, soon plucked up the tree by the roots. The affair created great excitement at the time and not a little ill feeling.

*Flushing Cemetery*—Was incorporated May 5th, 1853. It contains twenty-one acres, having a surface beautifully diversified and a soil well adapted to its purpose. It is situated one mile and a-half from the village, on the road to Fresh Meadows. It needs but the care and cultivation which affection for the departed is sure to call forth, from warm and loving hearts, to make it one of the most desirable sleeping places for the loved and lost.

*Town Poor House*—Was built in 1851. The farm is located at Fresh Meadows and contains forty-four acres. Average number of inmates, in 1860, twenty-four.

### VILLAGES, &C.

*Whitestone*, was settled at a very early date, probably about the same time with Flushing village. The name is derived from a large *white rock* (referred to in the patent) which lies off the point where the tides from East River and Long Island Sound meet. Many years ago, by a vote of the inhabitants at a public meeting, it was named Clintonville, after DeWitt Clinton; but in 1854 the old name Whitestone was restored, and a Post Office established. A. H. Kissam was the first Post Master, who was succeeded in 1857 by Charles H. Miller,

Part of the village of Whitestone is familiarly known as " Cookie Hill," from the following circumstance. Many years ago a cake and candy woman was carried away from New York, by accident, in a steamboat bound up the sound and was put ashore at this place. She, being disposed to make the best of her misfortune, walked boldly up to the town, and soon disposed of her toothsome stock to the idle crowd, among whom the incident was the subject of great mirth and gossip. "Cookie" is the Dutch word for cake, and this trifling occurrence, it appears, was sufficient to give a name to the locality.

Sixty years ago, within the circumference of one mile, there were only twelve houses in Whitestone, and no business was done until 1853, when a large establishment for the manufacture of japan, tin and copper ware was erected by John D. Locke & Co. This factory employs 150 hands. The population of the village in 1860 is about 800.

Several Hell Gate pilots have their residence here.

In the early part of the century there was a ferry at this point to Throgg's Neck. Its principal business was the conveyance of cattle. A sail boat was employed for the purpose, and H. Kissam was ferryman for fourteen years. Two years ago an unsuccessful attempt was made to re-establish this ferry.

Francis Lewis, one of the immortal signers of the Declaration of Independence, had a farm at Whitestone. He was the father of Hon. Morgan Lewis, one of the Governors of the State, and Major General U. S. A. in the war of 1812. The "Macedonian," after her engagement, lay off the point for several weeks with the sick and wounded.

*Strattonport—College Point.*—Eliphalet Stratton, some seventy years ago, purchased about three hundred and twenty acres of land in this locality for £500. About eight years ago his daughter, as trustee, sold that portion which now constitutes the village of Strattonport for $30,000, retaining the balance of one hundred and eighty acres in the family. College Point is the north westerly portion or that tract of land formerly known as Lawrence or Tew's Neck. Here was located St. Paul's College under the direction of Dr. Muhlenburgh. Its corner stone was laid by Bishop Onderdonk, October 15th, 1846. The Institution was particularly designed for the education of young men for the ministry of the Episcopal Church. With the discontinuance of the establishment the property passed into private hands. The College edifice is now used as a private residence. Divine Service has been held in the chapel during the summer season ever since the foundation of the College.

The village of Strattonport, or College Point, now contains two thousand inhabitants. Its rapid growth is due to the erection, in 1854, of a large factory by Popenhusen & Co., called the "Enterprise Works," for the manufacture of india rubber combs, knife handles and whalebone. This establishment in its various departments employs nearly five hundred hands. The Fire Department was organized in 1856, and consists of Hook and Ladder Company No. 1, H. L. C. Gieck, *Foreman*; and Union Engine Company No. 1, V. E. C. Felthauss *Foreman*.

The " Harmonie," a society for mutual benefit, has a library consisting of three hundred volumes. The Krakelia, a musical organization and two Turnvereins are also sustained.

The College Point Post Office was established in 1857, H. Zuberbier Post Master. Within the past three years several very costly villa residences have been erected in the northern portion of the village.

Perhaps it ill befits us to point out the delinquencies of our sister village, but a due regard for historical truth, compels us to add that a rigid observance of the Sabbath is not one of its commendable excellencies. Two theatres are said to be in full blast every Sunday evening, and its twelve Lager Beer Saloons, are reputed to do a thriving business on this day. This favorite beverage of the German, is here made. In the summer months not unfrequently do we see flags flying from its many places of public resort, hear bands of music, and occasionally listen to the tread of military visitors from the city, on the Sabbath day. Are such innovations upon our American customs consistent with the institutions of our land, or with the divine Law ?

To Dr. Muhlenburgh must be credited the first effort to shorten the distance to the Point, by the road across the meadows. He first constructed a plank walk, at his own expense. A road was afterwards built, but it was hardly in a fit condition for travel until the construction of the causeway in 1855.

*Little Neck.* The immediate lands surrounding Little Neck, possess many interesting reminiscences of the past. Relics of the Indian tribes are constantly found, and the innumerable quantity of shells found imbedded beneath the surface too truly denote the spots where the Warrior Chief and the aged Prophet rested in their wigwam, in fancied happy security. Perhaps the most interesting of these lands is the portion now known as "Douglass Point." These lands were first owned by one Thomas Hicks, long prior to the revolution, who forcibly seized them from the Indian tribes, then the occupants. They retired to the south side of the Island, and located in the vicinity of Springfield. They have become so mixed that scarce one of pure Indian descent can now be found. Stephen Burtis who resided at " Wigwam Pond," some sixty years ago, is the last known to be of strictly pure descendency. This pond, now known as Success Pond, is situated on the ridge of hills, forming part of the chain commonly called the "back bone" of Long Island. It has obtained much notoriety from the numerous fossil remains and Indian implements of war found in its vicinity. The old "tomb stones," now in the last stage of decay, in its immediate locality, are painfully indicative of the final resting place of the brave hearts of those who fought for that home of which they were the first possessors.

"Point Douglass" passed successively from Thomas Hicks to "Sheaf," a Hollander, thence to Thomas Weeks, by whom it was sold to Wynandt Van Zandt, who at his death bequeathed a portion to his children, by whom it was disposed of to its present owner, George Douglass.

Prior to 1821, the only road between Little Neck and Flushing was through what is now known as "the alley," serpentine and hilly and increasing the distance more than two miles before reaching its terminus at the corner known as the "Lonely Barn," near the residence of Mr. Ahlis. In 1824, the road from Little Neck Hotel was donated, the causeway constructed, and the bridge built by Mr. Van Zandt at his own expense. In 1834 the road was turnpiked under charter, to Roslyn, and three years subsequently as far eastward as Oyster Bay. A Post Office was established in 1859, J. A. Chapman Post Master.

"St. Ronan's Well." This singular wooded eminence, although not situated within the limits of our town is worthy of mention. It contains about twelve acres, and at high tide is entirely surrounded by water. In 1645 it was in the possession of Adrien Van der Donck, that distinguished "doctor of both laws." The Doctor was familiarly called the Yonker, a dutch title for a gentleman; and from this circumstance this piece of upland was known until recently as Yonker's Island. Afterward it was called " Snake Hill." For many years it has been a favorite place of resort for target and pic-nic excursions from the city and elsewhere.

# CHAPTER V.

The old Bowne House on Bowne Avenue was erected in 1661, by the first John Bowne. It has oak flooring, fastened to the beams by oak pins. In one of its rooms the early Friends held their meetings for nearly forty years. The family possess a number of interesting relics of antiquity, an old fashioned clock reaching from the ceiling to the floor, and still preaching as impressively as two hundred years ago, its solemn sermon of time's rapid flight; a lounge on which the celebrated George Fox rested after his fatiguing labors when on his visit to Flushing in 1672 : (will modern lounges wear as long ?) ; an old table with legs of a thickness surprising to modern eyes, from which the Friends at their Quarterly Meetings have often-times partaken of " the good things of this life ;" an old Bible, in black letter type, dated 1622, and a scrap book, in which are preserved a large number of manuscript letters, and papers, of which one is dated 1622, two hundred and thirty-six years old.

In repairing the house a few years since a hole was discovered in one of the walls, which had been plastered over, and in which doubtless valuables were once concealed. Yet this old house has been subjected to modern innovations, being heated by a furnace and illuminated by gas.

Near by is another venerable relic, the large oak tree, known as the " Fox Oak," which is supposed to be about four hundred years old. Another formerly stood a short distance from it. As companions they had stood side by side, and bade defiance to the fierceness of the tempest and the stroke of the thunderbolt. For centuries not an angry word passed between them, not a sullen look had darkened the brow of either. Their huge arms had been outstretched toward each other only for friendly embrace. But on 25th October, 1841, one of these sturdy brothers bowed his head and passed away.

Here we must be permitted to insert the following articles, written at the time, by fellow towns- men and published in the first number of the Flushing Journal.

Thompson in his history of Long Island, ascribes the first to Col. Wm. L. Stone, Editor of the New York Commercial Advertiser, not a little complimentary to its true author, James B. Parsons. It is headed

"A VETERAN GONE."

" The oldest inhabitant of Flushing, is no more. During the afternoon of the 25th inst. one of the

venerable oaks, which for so many centuries have
been a prominent object in Bowne Avenue, near
the village of Flushing, was prostrated to the
ground. To a stranger, this contains no higher
occasion for regret than the removal of a noble
tree, by the operation of the inevitable laws of
nature; but to those who have passed many a
happy hour of childhood in gathering the acorns
which fell from it, and have made it the scene of
of their youthful sports, it seems like the removal
of a venerated relative, as if one of the few visible
links, which in this utilitarian land connects us
with the past, was severed."

To the members of the Society of Friends, these
trees possessed a historical interest, from the circumstance that beneath them about the year 1673,
the dauntless founder of their sect,* with that power and eloquence of truth, which drew to his standard Penn and Barclay and a host of men like them,
preached the Gospel of Redemption to a mixed
assemblage, among which might be seen many a
son of the swarthy family, whose wrongs and sufferings elicit to this day the active efforts of his

---

* George Fox, in his wonderful journal, thus speaks of his visit to
Flushing:

"1672." From Oyster Bay we passed about thirty miles to Flushing, where we had a very large meeting, many hundreds of people
being there; some of whom came about thirty miles to it. A glorious
and heavenly meeting it was (praised be the Lord God!) and the people were much satisfied.

followers on their behalf. Some seventy years since these honored trees were threatened with demolition by the owner of the adjacent property ; but for the sake of the venerable past were purchased by John Bowne, a lineal descendant of the old worthy of the same name, who listened to the preaching of Fox and embraced his doctrines, for which he was afterwards sent to Holland in irons, where he was honorably liberated by the Dutch Government, and a severe reprimand administered to Stuyvesant. The time-honored mansion, in which he entertained Fox, and accommodated the regular meetings of the Society for many years, is still standing and in good repair.—Oct. 25th, 1841.

The other article is by Samuel B. Parsons, and is entitled

### "THE FLUSHING OAK."

" The Ancient Oak lies prostrate now,
    Its limbs embrace the sod,
Where in the Spirit's strength and might
    Our pious fathers trod ;
Where underneath its spreading arms
    And by its shadows broad,
Clad in simplicity and truth,
    They met to worship God.

" No stately pillars round them rose,
    No dome was reared on high ;
The oaks their only columns were,
    Their roof the arching sky ;

No organ's deep-toned notes arose,
　Or vocal songs were heard ;
Their music was the passing wind,
　Or song of forest bird.

" And as His Spirit reached their hearts,
　By man's lips speaking now,
A holy fire was in their eye,
　Pure thought upon their brow ;
And while in silence deep and still,
　Their souls all glowing were
With heart-felt peace and joy and love,
　They felt that God was there.

" Those pure and simple minded men,
　Have now all passed away,
And of the scenes in which they moved,
　These only relics lay ;
And soon the last surviving oak,
　In its majestic pride,
Will gather up its failing limbs,
　And wither at its side.

" Then guard with care its last remains,
　Now that its race is run ;
No sacriligious hand should touch
　The forest's noblest one ;
And when the question may be asked,
　Why that old trunk is there ;
'Tis but the place, in olden time,
　God's holiest altars were."

The old Quaker meeting house, still in good preservation and used for religious meetings, was erected in 1695, and bears the marks of revolutionary occupancy. .

The small building near the dwelling of G. R. Garretson, on a line with the street, is supposed to be nearly as old as the Bowne house. It was formerly one of the principal stores in the village, and was afterwards used jointly as a drug store and a silversmith shop. It is now occupied by Mr. Garretson as a seed storehouse.

The old "Guard House" to which frequent reference is made in various records, and which we shall have occasion to mention hereafter, was a long, low, frame building, erected originally for purposes of defence, and used ultimately as a town jail. It stood at the corner of Union street and Broadway.

The Whipping-post, an institution of the olden time, at which many a poor *fellow* expiated the crime of stealing and such minor offences against the majesty of the law, stood nearly opposite the Flushing Hotel, a few feet from the present curb stone. It was abolished fifty years ago.

Another object of interest, about which every stranger, upon coming into the village, is sure to make enquiries, is that noble specimen of architecture, with splendid columns upholding its portico, with one room about sixteen by twenty feet, for the accommodation of the village Aldermen, and with its four smaller rooms underneath for the accommodation of those who need the restraints of law. The *Village Hall*, while it was eminently creditable to the enterprise and liberality of the citizens, and answered all the necessities of the place at the time of its erection, is now wholly inadequate to our wants. It is itself a *standing appeal* to our enterprising citizens for its demolition, and the erection in its room of a building which will furnish accommodations for the Board of Trustees; a place for holding elections; a hall for public lectures; rooms for Lyceum purposes, Library, &c. We know of no place of the size and wealth of Flushing which is not provided with something of this kind. Efforts have indeed been made from time to time to effect this object, but hitherto without success. We trust the day is not far distant when we shall be able to point with becoming pride to a *Village Hall* worthy of our beautiful village, and commensurate with our wants. We scarcely know of any one thing by which our men of means could do more for the intellectual and moral benefit of the place, than by uniting their efforts and liberality, and determining that this "consummation so devoutly to be wished for" shall be reached

ST MICHAELS CATHOLIC CHURCH

One of the most beautiful characteristics of our village is the great number of ornamental trees that adorn its streets, and the grounds and gardens of its residents. This generation does, and succeeding ones will, hold in grateful remembrance those public-spirited individuals, who originated and have encouraged this branch of home industry and internal improvements. We trust this work will be continued, and that not a street will be opened without these adornments studding its walks. It was commenced about forty years ago, by Samuel Parsons, father of the Messrs. Parsons.* With his own hand he planted the first shade trees along the Bay Side road. His example was followed extensively, and the result is

* Samuel Parsons is represented to us as "a fine specimen of a Christian gentleman, of polished manners, and liberal classical education. His benevolent and religious qualities were such that he was always in demand when trouble, sickness or death came upon the villagers. No one probably ever lived in the place more generally marked and beloved than he." That such was his character, I find supported by the testimony of all of whom I have made enquiry who were acquainted with him, and cherish his memory. I will therefore, be pardoned for quoting a few lines which record with filial tenderness the grateful remembrance of a father's worth.

"Our Father was so thoroughly imbued
With all the Christian graces, grafted on
A nature gentle as a woman's soul,
That all the people loved him, and they came
To him for counsel, and they sent for him
When death's dark shadows gathered o'er their heads,

seen in the beauty of our place. Without these it would be shorn of much of its attractiveness.

---

For well they knew that with the Holy One
He held communion ; and in silent awe,
They listened to his fervent loving prayers
That faith in Christ, and in his wondrous love,
Might light the pathway of the dying one,
And lead him to the realms of endless day.
And sometimes, in a twilight hour like this,
He'd gather us around him, kneel in prayer,
And pour out for us such beseeching words,
That all the room seemed full of Angel's wings,
And, to our youthful hearts, a Presence seemed
Hovering around, as visible to sense
As the Shekinah which the Hebrew saw."

# CHAPTER VI.

PERSONAL INCIDENTS—REMINISCENCES--REV. FRAN-
CIS DOUGHTY, CAPT. JOHN UNDERHILL, REUBEN
BOWEN, AND OTHERS.

In this chapter our original purpose was to have
given a brief sketch of those whose names are
found in the charter of incorporation, and whose
descendants are still living among us. But we find
the materials so scanty, at least such as we can
collect in the limited time at our command, that we
have abandoned that intention, and present such
as we have under another form. For many of
the facts stated we are indebted to papers collected by Peter S. Townsend, M. D., and now in possession of Robert Townsend, Esq., of Albany, who
kindly permitted us their use.

Rev. Francis Doughty. Some obscurity exists
concerning this person. The following is the most
connected account we can gather :—

It appears he " came to New England at the
commencement of the troubles in England, and
found that he had got out of the frying pan into
the fire." He seemes to have preached at Taun-
ton, Mass., and " for declaring that Abraham
ought to have been baptised," he was by order of
10

the Magistrates dragged by the Constables out of the public assembly, and soon after was compelled to leave with his children.

He also preached at Linn, Mass., where he denied baptism to infants. This doctrine could not be tolerated in that puritanical atmosphere.

He consequently betook himself to New Netherlands. He settled at Mespath, Long Island, and as agent for some families who were to follow, obtained a patent, "with manorial privileges," of considerable land of which he was to have "a bouerie" in return for his services as Preacher, and from which he was to obtain his living. About one year after his settlement began, war broke out, and the colony was scattered. He, with most of the colony, went to the city, and ministered there. After peace was established he was required to return, which, after some time, he did, and remained half a year, when he again removed.

In 1645, or soon after, he became the minister at Vlissengen. A few years subsequently he had some difficulty with them touching the amount of his salary.

In a Report to Classis of Amsterdam, dated Aug. 5th, 1657, by Revds. John Megapolensis and Samuel Drisius, they say, " At Flushing they heretofore had a Presbyterian Preacher who

conformed to our Church, but many of them became endowed with divers opinions, and it was
with them *quot homines tot Sententiæ*. They ab-
sented themselves from preaching, nor would they
pay the Preacher his promised stipend. The said
preacher was obliged to leave the place and to
repair to the English Virginias." "Last year a
fomenter of errors came there. He began to
preach at Flushing and then went with the people
into the river and dipped them." He was arrested and banished the province. Which of these
two refers to Rev. Mr Doughty we can not de-
termine. The Baptist views would indicate the
latter; but the dates, the removal to Virginia,
and the refusal to pay, point to the former, which
we are inclined to favor.

In 1653—4 we find him before the Bergomas-
ter's Court, in New Netherlands, in an action
versus John Lawrence, defendant, with reference
to his salary as Clergyman. He is dissatisfied
with the amount paid him and declares what was
promised to him. He is recommended to lay his
case before the Director-General and Council. In
1656 he went to Virginia, and in 1659 he was in
Maryland.

What became of him is not known. He was
unquestionably the first religious teacher in Flushing, and had adopted Baptist views of the ordi

nance of Baptism. He was the progenitor of the Doughty family on the Island.

John Marston, Sr. His will is dated Feb. 14th, 1670—1. "I will my two sons, John and Cornelius, to my well beloved friend John Hinchman,* to live with him, and to be wholly at his disposing, till they come of age according to law." After payment of his debts the estate all goes to his two sons, "Except one gold ring and one silver thimble. I give to my daughter Elizabeth the ring, and to my daughter Catharine the thimble."

Wm. Thorne Jr. purchased the land called after him, Thorne's Neck, afterwards called Willet's Point, and lately sold to the Government of the United States. He is the progenitor of this numerous and respectable family. He removed from Sandwich, Mass. to Flushing in 1642. Tradition gives him two brothers. One of them settled at Cow Neck, and was an enthusiastic sportsman, bringing his hounds with him from England. Walking over his fields one day, dejected and melancholy, it is supposed, over his difficulties and prospects in the new world, he committed suicide by twisting a sapling round his neck.

---

* He was first owner of a large estate at Bay-Side which he sold to Thomas Hicks, Junr.

Edward Ffarrington was brother-in-law of John Bowne. His will is dated " 14th day of the 4th month, 1673." He wills, after the decease of his wife Dorothy, to his " eldest son John," all his ' housing, land, orchard, gardens in the town of Fflushing, &c, to returne to the next heire, male, of the blood of the Ffarringtons, and soe from generation to generation for ever." The pride and prejudice in favor of primogeniture are very conspicuous.

Captain John Underhill. This famous individual, " one of the most dramatic persons in our early history," came from England to Massachusetts, shortly after the commencement of the colony. He appears to have been of a bold, daring, restless, reckless temper, and was in almost constant difficulties, sometimes with the church, sometimes with the government. He was frequently employed in the engagements between the whites and the Indians. He was in the war against the Block Islanders, and received an arrow through his coat and another against the helmet, on his forehead—which helmet he was induced to wear by the advice of his wife: "therefore" he says, " let no man despise the advice and counsel of his wife, *though she be a woman.* It were strange to nature to think a man should be bound to fulfil the humour of a woman, what arms he should carry, but you know God will have it so, that a woman should overcome a man. What with Delilah's flattery, and with her mournful tears, they must, and will have their desire." He was excommunicated upon his own confession of adultery, but by his repeated confessions, many tears and prayers was restored to membership and released from banishment.

In 1644 he came to Long Island, and for a time resided in Flushing. He wanted military employment. But as the colonies refused to take part in the difficulties between England and Holland, he applied to Rhode Island, which gave a commission to him and William Dyre "to go against the Dutch, or any enemies of the commonwealth of England." A guard of soldiers was sent by the Dutch authorities to apprehend him; but he promised to be faithful to the Dutch, and was thereupon set at liberty. In 1667 the Matinecock Indians conveyed to him a large tract of their lands. A part of this, appropriately named Killingworth, situate at Oyster Bay, remained in the family for nearly two hundred years. He died in 1672.

We find the following quaint, interesting, and characteristic declaration of Independence, which must have been proclaimed about the time of his commission by Rhode Island, to fight the Dutch :

" May 20th, after the birth of Christ 1653.

" *Vindication* of Capt. John Underhill in the name of as many Dutch and English as the matter concerns, which justly compels us to renounce the iniquitous government of Peter Stuyvesant, over the inhabitants living and dwelling on Long Island, in America.

" We declare that it is right and proper to defend ourselves and our rights, which belong to a free people, against the abuse of the above named government.

" We have transported ourselves hither at our cost, and many among us have purchased their lands from the Indians, the right owners thereof. But a great portion of the lands which we occupy, being, as yet, unpaid for, the Indians come daily and complain that they have been deceived by the Dutch Secretary, called Cornelus, whom they have characterized, even in the presence of Stuyvesant, as a rogue, a knave, and a liar; asserting that he himself had put their names down in the book, and saying that this was not a just and lawful payment, but a pretence and fraud similar to that which occasioned the destruction of Jo⁰ˢ Hutchinsen and Mr. Collins, to the number of nine persons.

"III. He hath unlawfully retained from several persons their lands which they had purchased from the natives, and which were confirmed to them under the hand and seal of the previous Governor.

"IV. He hath unlawfully imposed taxes contrary to the privileges of free men; namely, six stivers per acre, chimney money and head money; the tenth part of all our grain, flax, hemp and tobacco; the tenth part of butter and cheese from those who pasture cattle; excessive duties on exported goods, fifteen stivers for a beaver; all of which taxes are to be paid by the poor farmers to maintain a lazy horde of tyrants over innocent subjects.

"V. He hath, in violation of liberty of conscience, and contrary to hand and seal, enforced articles upon the people, ordering them otherwise, against the laws of God and Man, to quit the country within two months.

"VI. He hath imprisoned both English and Dutch, without trial, setting them at liberty again, after the manner of a Popish inquisition to their great Sorrow, damage and loss of time, himself not having any patent from James, King of England, the right grantor thereof.

"VII. He hath also imposed general laws forbidding the inhabitants to sell their goods or to brew their grain, without the approbation of the government.

" VIII. He hath neglected to avenge English and Dutch blood shed by the Indians since the peace.

" IX. He hath treacherously and undoubtedly conspired, as proved, to murder all the English.

" X. He hath been guilty of barbarous cruelty towards Mr. Jacob Wolfertsen and his wife, at the time of the birth of their child.

" XI. He hath acted treacherously towards Thomas Miton, for, notwithstanding the government hath promised him safe and secure conduct, he hath ordered his arrest and extradition.

" XII. He hath been guilty of the unheard-of act of striking, with his cane, an old gentleman, a member of his Council, and had publicly threatened every freeman who does not conform to his pleasure.

" XIII. He hath, moreover, imposed magistrates on freemen without election and voting. This great autocracy and tyranny is too grievous for any brave Englishman and good Christian any longer to tolerate. In addition to all this, the Dutch have proclaimed war against every Englishman who live wherever *he may wish or like.*

" The above grounds are sufficient for all honest hearts that seek the glory of God and their own peace and prosperity, to throw off this tyrannical yoke. Accept and submit ye, then, to the Parliament of England, and beware ye of becoming traitors to one another, for the sake of your own quiet and welfare.

Written by me,

JOHN UNDERHILL."

Michael Milnor. It was at his house that the Flushing people met to draw up the famous remonstrance, which we have elsewhere given, against the oppressive acts of Gov. Stuyvsant towards the Quakers.

Jonathan Wright, Sr. The only notice we have seen of him is that he had children, named as follows :—Jonathan, David, John, Charles, Job, Samuel, Richard, Henry, George, Elizabeth, Sarah, Mary, Hannah.

Richard Cornell was Justice of the Peace at Flushing, Feb. 17th, 1668.

Wm. Hallett was Scout or Constable, in 1668. The inhabitants presented to the Governor General the following petition :—

" Right Honorable, Wee your humble petitioners, having some hopes and confidence in your clemency and favor, are boulde to present you with a few lines in behalf of our Scout, Mr. William Hallett, &c." And particularly, it would appear, in behalf of his children who " depend on him for meate, drinke, and clothing, &c.;" " the man having great loss in the late warres, therefore out of human pity and commisseration wee are boulde to supplicate your honor, for his release and acquittance, what offence he hath committed wee are ignorant of, therefore we can neither justifye nor condemn. However we take you for the preserver of our liberties, and if through weakness wee doe offend wee hope you will be instructive, not destructive to us. Therefore as christian petitioners wee despaire not to find peace and favor from you and humbly desire your Lordship to have compassion on our friend and neighbour with respect to his family, and we shall ever, &c."

But the petition was unsuccessful, and the Scout was banished March 9th, 1648. His crime was it is said, adultery.

John, William, and Thomas Lawrence, three brothers, of which John was the eldest, were among the earliest English settlers on Long Island. Thomas, the youngest brother, by purchase from the Dutch settlers, became proprietor of the whole of Hell-gate, where he resided, and from whom the Newtown branch of the family have descended.

John soon removed from Flushing to New Amsterdam, where he held various important public stations, both under the Dutch and English rule He died in 1699, when over eighty years of age

William continued to reside at Flushing during his life. He was a very extensive landed proprietor; and at his death his sword, plate, and other personals, were valued at £4,432 sterling. He was a man of superior mind, liberal education, great energy and decision of character, as his letters to Stuyvesant and council show. He held civil and military offices under both Dutch and English. His descendants are very numerous. Part of his lands are now occupied by descendents from his third son Joseph, by his second wife, viz :—James, Wm. Augustus, and Charles Crummeline Lawrence. From his first son, William, by his first wife, are descended Judge Effingham W. Lawrence and Hon. John W. Lawrence, whose father seems to have left Flushing at an early age, returned in 1794, and purchased the property where his sons now reside.

The residence of the first Wm. Lawrence was at Lawrence's or Tew's Neck. He died in 1680. His son Joseph, mentioned above, while residing

---

We do not give a more detailed genealogy of the Lawrence family, as it is given in full in works expressly devoted to it, and accessible to all interested in the matter. There must have existed a very strong conservative element in the family to have preserved so large a landed property among them through several generations, in this country, where lands are not entailed. It certainly manifests a stability of character not frequently observed in our population.

on his estate, on Little Neck Bay, became intimate with Lord Effingham, a commander of a British frigate, anchored in the Sound, near his mansion. In compliment to so distinguished a stranger, his grandson was named Effingham. This, we believe, was the introduction of that name in the family.

John Bowne was born at Matlock in Derbyshire, England, in 1627. He came to Boston in 1649, and shortly after settled at Flushing. He married in 1656, Hannah, daughter of Robert Field, and sister of the wife of Capt. John Underhill. His wife attended the meetings of the Quakers, and within a short time joined the Society. He soon followed her example. For adhering to the Society and attending their meetings, he was arrested, tried and fined twenty-five Flemish pounds; and refusing to pay, was cast into prison, and at length, in 1663, was transported to Holland, "for the welfare of community, and to crush as far as it is possible that abominable sect, who treat with contempt both the political magistrates and the ministers of God's holy word, and endeavor to undermine the police and religion." Upon "manifesting his case" to the West India Company, at Amsterdam, they did not utter "one word tending to the approval of any thing" that had been done by way of religious persecution. In

11

their next despatch to Gov. Stuyvesant they rebuked him as follows :—" Although it is our desire that similar and other sectarians may not be found there, yet as the contrary seems to be the fact, we doubt very much whether rigorous proceedings against them ought not to be discontinued; unless, indeed, you intend to check and destroy your population, which, in the youth of your existence, ought rather to be encouraged by all possible means. Wherefore, it is our opinion that some connivance is useful, and that at least the consciences of men ought to remain free and unshackled. Let every one remain free as long as he is modest, moderate, his political conduct irreproachable, and as long as he does not offend others or oppose the government. This maxim of moderation has always been the guide of our magistrates in this city ; and the consequence has been that people have flocked from every land to this asylum. Tread thus in their steps, and we doubt not you will be blessed." Ah ! those liberal-minded, far-seeing Dutchmen in the Fatherland, amid all the clouds which rolled up gracefully as " divinest incense" from their smoking pipes, understood the value of civil and religious liberty ; and they maintained it too at a sacrifice of treasure and a baptism of blood, such as no other nation has ever paid for a like priceless possession.

The following paper, without date or direction, was doubtless presented at some stage in these proceedings, probably, to the West India Company, in the year 1662.

"*Friends*—The paper drawn up for me to subscribe I have perused and weighed, and doe find the same not according to that engagement to me through one of your members (viz) that hee or you would doe therein by me as you would be done unto, and noe otherwise. Ffor which of you being taken by force from your wife and ffamillie (without just case) would be bound from returning to them, unlesse upon termes to Act Contrarie to your Consciences, deny your faith and Religion, yet to this (in effect) doe you require of mee and noe lesse. But truly I can not think that you did in sober earnest ever think that I would subscribe to any such thing; it being the very thing for which I rather chuse freely to suffer want of the Company of my dear wife and children, imprisonment of my person, and the ruien of my estate in my absence there, and the losse of my goods here, than to yield or consent unto such an unreasonable thing, as you thereby would injoyn mee unto; ffor which I am persuaded, you will not only be judged in the sight of God, but by good and Godly men, rather to have mocked at the oppressions of the oppressed and added afflictions to the afflicted, than herein to have done to mee, as you in the like case would be done unto, which the Royal Law of our God requires.

"I have with patience and moderation waited severall weekes, expecting Justice from you, but behold an addition to my oppression is the measure I receive. Wherefore I have this now to request for you, that the Lord will not lay this to your charge, but to give eyes to see, and hearts to doe Justice, that you may find mercy with the Lord in the day of Judgment.

JOHN BOWNE."

The exile returned to his home after an absence of two years, and persecution ceased in New Netherlands.

His wife, who was a preacher in the Society, left for England on a preaching tour in 1675. He followed her in 1676. She died in 1677. Shortly after he returned and married a second time in 1679. This wife died in 1690. He married a third wife in 1693. He died in 1695, aged sixty-eight years. After his death, the Society at their yearly meeting, made this record : " he did abundance of good, and died beloved by all sorts of people."

Six John Bownes have successively occupied the "old Bowne house;" the last dying in 1804, aged sixty-four years. Ann Bowne, a daughter of the last, still resides in the family mansion.

Here we may relate an anecdote of the first John Bowne, which tradition has preserved in the family. He was journeying with a brother Friend to the city. At some point along the road when passing a piece of woods, a huge black bear rushed out of the thicket with an evident intention of regaling his palate with the blood and flesh of the non-resisting Friends. But Bowne had no thought of being so summarily served up. So on the principle of self defence he watched Bruin's approach and thrust his cane down the throat of his antagonist, who had murder in his looks, with such efficient though Quakerly force that after a moment's struggle, poor Bruin fell and expired.

Francis Bloodgood. Among the Dutch families, who very early settled at Flushing, was the Bloodgood, January 13th 1776. Letters of administration were granted by Gov. Andros to Elizabeth, wife of Francis Bloodgood, of Flushing.

The following account of this person and his descendants is condensed from a statement furnished by Simeon De Witt Bloodgood, Esq., of

11*

New York, and by Dr. Abr'm Bloodgood of Flushing. He emigrated from Holland, but in what year is not known. In Sept. 1673 he was chosen Magistrate of Flushing. March 22d, 1674; "a Commission was this day given by the Governor General to Francis Bloetgoet, *Chief* of the inhabitants of the Dutch Nation residing in the Villages Vlissengen, Heemstede, Rusdorp and Middlebergh, and the places belonging to these districts, by which the aforesaid F. B. is Commanded to Communicate to said inhabitants that they on the first notice of the enemy's arrival, or on the arrival of more ships than one, at once shall march well armed towards the city upon the penalty," &c. A farther commission was issued to him to sit as "Privy Counsellor," in consultation with the Governor as to the surrender of the colony to the English. He was also appointed Commissioner to visit the Swedish settlement on the Delaware. From these facts it is evident he was a man of no little distinction.

Of his next immediate descendents little is known. He had grandchildren, Abram and James. At an early age they were left orphans under the care of a relative, but made their way in the world for themselves. They emigrated to Albany, engaged in business and accumulated handsome fortunes.

Abraham was born in 1741 in the town of Flushing. He became a merchant in Albany, and married Mrs. Lynott, who had two daughters at the time; one of whom married the celebrated Simeon De Witt. He was frequently elected to the Common Council of Albany—was a member of the Convention which accepted the Constitution of the United States, and was one of ten who met in the old Vanden Heyden House, in Pearl street, and founded the Democratic party of this State. He had *four sons*, Francis, James, Lynott and Joseph. The latter chose the Medical profession. He graduated from the University of Pennsylvania in 1806, and was appointed Trustee of the College of Physicians and Surgeons of New York in 1811. Upon the strength of an invitation from a number of the most prominent citizens of Flushing he came to this place in 1812. He was for many years an eminent practitioner. He died March 7th, 1851, aged sixty-seven years six months and twenty-one days. He had four daughters, one married Wm. Boardman, formerly minister of the Presbyterian church at Newtown, Long Island. He had eight sons, Abraham, Isaac, Joseph, William, Frances, Lynott, John T. and De Witt C. Four only are living, Isaac, William, John and Abraham.

# CHAPTER VII.

## SCHOOLS—INSTITUTIONS—NURSERIES AND NEWSPAPERS.

*Schools.*—Of the early schools I have obtained but little information. Lindley Murray Moore kept a school for several years, in a building which stood on the site of the present Flushing Hotel. He left about 1827, and was succeeded by the late Joshua Kimber; he was succeeded by William Chase, who relinquished the school in 1858. A school was also kept, we are informed, for many years in the old Friends' meeting house.

The old Lecture Room of the Episcopal church, lately removed, was built for an academy, and was the first in the village. It cost $1,250. The expense, we learn from William R. Prince, was borne mainly by five persons, viz :—Hutchins Smith, (father of D. Thorne Smith,) William Prince, John Aspinwall and two others whose names are not known. In this building, William A. Houghton, now of New York, taught a school from 1819 to 1825.

Rev. Charles Carpenter, a Methodist minister, kept a boarding and day school about four years,

W<sup>m</sup>. Momberger. Lith NY

FLUSHING INSTITUTE.

from 1820 to 1824. He resided in the old Farrington house, and his school-room was in Washington Street, a few doors above James Ewbank's
store.

*Flushing Institute.*—This was incorporated
April 16th 1827. The corner stone of the edifice
was laid August 23d, 1827. It contained a Greek
Testament, Newspapers, names of county officers
etc. It was at first occupied by Rev. Dr. William
A. Muhlenburg for ten years as a school for boys.
Then under the name of St. Ann's Hall, it was a
school for young ladies of which Rev. Dr. Schroe-
der was principal. It was again changed into a
school for young gentlemen, under the principal-
ship of the late Elias Fairchild. His son, E. A,
Fairchild, still continues it, as principal and proprietor. The success which has crowned his
earnest, well-directed efforts attests its character
for instruction and discipline.

*St. Thomas Hall.*—This was erected by Rev.
Francis L. Hawks in 1839. His buildings and arrangements were probably as perfect as ever were
designed for such purposes. Connected with the
present edifices, formerly, was a large circular brick
building having eight school-rooms with small re-
citation rooms and other conveniences. The doors
were constructed of glass. In the centre was an
elevated platform, which commanded a view of

all the class rooms. A circular stairs led to the
dome of the building, up which refractory boys
were sent. Dr. Hawks relinquished it in 1843.
It remained vacant about a year. The property
was then purchased by Gerardus Beekman Docherty, L. L. D. and Dr. Carmichael, then of Hempstead. The latter remained about a year. Dr.
Docherty continued until 1848. Rev. Wm. H.
Gilder purchased and took possession July 1st,
1848. It is now a regularly chartered Female
College, being one of three in the State. It con-
fers degrees and diplomas to those young ladies who
pursue the entire course of study as prescribed.*

The late Jemima Hammond had a private
school for several years in her residence in Ailanthus place.

In the same building Mrs. Sarah K. Roberts
now conducts a school designed both for young
ladies and small children.†

Miss Blake has also successfully conducted a
school for young children, in the Lecture Room
of the Methodist Church.

In the Fall of 1859, Rev. Henry Dana Ward,
and Mrs. Ward opened a school for young ladies
in the building on the corner of State and Linnæus
Streets.

---

* Since writing the above this school has been discontinued.

† Mrs. Roberts has since removed to the commodious building on
the corner of State and Farrington Streets.

*Public School.*—The system of Free Schools originated in Geneva, and in parishes of Scotland. John Calvin was "the father of popular education. It is the glory of our Fathers to have established in the laws the equal claims of every child to the *public* care of its morals and its mind."*

The only Public School in Flushing for many years was that under the care and patronage of the "Flushing Female Association." This useful society was organized Feb. 2d, 1814. The school was opened in a dwelling which stood near the site of the present school-house, in Liberty street, April 6th, 1814, with nineteen scholars. It was at first taught gratuitously by members of the Association in turn, two serving at a time. This plan was not long continued. In the report of July 1st, 1814, it is stated a teacher had been engaged at a salary of sixty dollars per annum, with two dollars a week for board; the members visiting in turn, two a week. The first examination occurred June 10th, 1815, " to the satisfaction of the audience, several being present from the city of New York, one of whom evinced his entire approbation by transmitting a donation of twenty dollars to the institution, and ten dollars to the teacher, for her becoming behaviour on the

* George Bancroft.

occasion." It was first supported by voluntary contributions; the scholars, both white and colored, being admitted free of charge, except a few whose parents were able and willing to pay. Oct. 1st, 1829 the scholars were required to pay two cents a week. It has received assistance from the state. The prosperity of the school has varied, at times over one hundred have been in attendance. At times it has been closed altogether; once for twenty months. When the present Public School was opened this was closed, but was reopened the following year. Since April 1st, 1855, it has been in charge of the trustees of the Public School, the association meanwhile retaining its special care and oversight. It is now exclusively for colored children. Its annual rent is about three hundred dollars, derived from the trustees of the Public School, fees of its members, and interest on the following bequests :—

Thomas Tom,  - - - - -  $250

Thomas Lawrence,  - - - -  100

Matthew Franklin,  - - - -  £150, " the interest to be applied to the use of finding poor negro children books, and also toward paying their schooling, them that their parents did belong among the people called Quakers."

Nathaniel Smith,  - - - -  $500

James Byrd,  - - - - - -  200

Charles and Scott Hicks furnished wood for the school, gratuitously, from its first year to 1825.

The present school-building was erected in 1819, at a cost of $844 73.

In 1844 the school, of which we have just given an account, was considered unequal to the necessities of the place. The public funds were therefore taken from it, and another school established in a new school-house. But the attempt was a failure. "Parents would not send their children to this school, nor did they feel able to pay for their education at any of the private schools." Another effort was made. Several public meetings were held. Much discussion ensued. Dec. 26th, 1847, at a public meeting it was resolved, by a vote of thirty-seven to five, to raise three thousand dollars by tax, and to authorize the trustees to sell the old building, to contract for a new one on the plan of the New York public schools, and to report a suitable site. Jan. 4th, 1848 a second meeting was held. The question upon changing the site was proposed and lost. This in reality reversed the action of the preceding meeting. Feb. 4th another meeting was held, nearly all the legal voters of the district being present. This, by a vote of ninety-nine to fifty eight, sustained the action of the first meeting. The Legislature was petitioned, and an act was passed authorizing

" the Board to raise six thousand and five hundred dollars by tax or mortgage for the erection of a building, and limiting the annual assessment to one-fifth of one per cent. on all the taxable property in the District." March 29th this act was approved by a vote of one hundred and forty to eighty-seven. June 13th a plan and estimate for building was presented and adopted, and at a subsequent meeting the present site on Union street was ordered to be purchased. July 18th ground was broken. Nov. 27th, 1848, the school was opened with seven teachers and three hundred and thirty-one scholars. Previous to this time in all the schools of the village there were in attendance only two hundred and thirteen children. It has been in successful operation to the present time. An Evening School was started in the winter of 1859. It numbered fifty-one scholars.

*Board of Education.*—E. E. Mitchell, S. B. Parsons, George C. Baker, C. H. Hamilton and C. W. Cox. Number of teachers, nine. Number of pupils, three hundred and sixty-seven.

*St. Michael's Catholic School*—The following statement of this school was furnished by the present Pastor, Rev. James O'Bierne :—Was organized Aug. 1st, 1853, under the patronage of Rev. John McMahon, then Pastor. For some time previous the Catholics of Flushing were beginning to tire of the Public School for which they were heavily taxed, and in which, of course, it was impossible their children could receive any religious instruction. The Sunday School, too, was found to be entirely insufficient for that purpose. The parents were in many cases unable, and in most cases unwilling to instruct their children at home; and thus it was, that the children were growing up, not only ignorant of the mysteries and tenets of their own Faith, but indifferent to every form of religious belief. Such was pretty much the state of the Catholic mind in Flushing, when an incident occurred, trifling in itself, but which led to a total rupture with the Public School. One of the Catholic children when saying her night prayers aloud for her mother, added to the Lord's prayer, " For thine is the kingdom, &c. &c " which is not found in the Catholic Bible. The mother became alarmed, and reported the matter to the Rev. John McMahon, who wrote to one of the Public School trustees, requesting that the Catholic children might not be required to be present at the reading of the Protestant bible. This request, it was stated, could not be granted. Immediately a meeting of the Catholics was held, and it was unanimously resolved to build a schoolhouse as soon as possible. In the course of a few weeks funds were raised, and the present school-house was built. The average attandance is about three hundred children. The school is entirely a free school. There are three teachers whose salary amounts to about nine hundred dollars per year. Besides the usual branches taught in the school, the children receive religious instruction every day; many of them also receive lessons in vocal and instrumental music on two days of the week. At first it was supposed, even by some Catholics, that the school would prove a failure, and that the children would again return to the Public School, but the supposition proved to be groundless. The school is at present in a most prosperous condition.

In 1857 a Public School was established in Whitestone. Though strongly opposed in its commencement, it is now firmly established and prosperous. It employs four female teachers. The average number of scholars in attendance is one hundred and seventy. The alteration and enlargement of the building cost fifteen hundred dollars. The night school has forty pupils. J. D. Locke, Esq., with characteristic liberality, pays one dollar for each pupil from his factory. Not a little credit is due to those who originated and established this enterprise; Messrs. Samuel L. Shotwell (teacher,) A. H. Kissam, T. H. Leggett, C. H. Miller, J. Fowler, H. Lowerree, &c.

College Point Public School.—This was organized in 1859, and employs three male and female teachers, and has an average attendance of one hundred and fifty scholars. The first night school established in this town was in connection with this school.

Of schools in other parts of the town we have not been able to gather statistics.

*Nurseries.*—The first nursery, called "the Linnæan Botanic Garden," was commenced by Wm. Prince, about 1737. This garden had two entrances, one in front of his residence, which was the long one and a-half story, round shingled house in Lawrence street, the other on the south side of Bridge street, about where E. Krieg's furniture store now stands. At the time the Revolution broke out his business was so extensive that three thousand cherry trees, for which there was then no sale, were cut down and sold for hoop-poles. When the British troops entered Flushing Gen. Howe stationed a guard of troops at both gates to protect the property from depredation; and this was continued as long as their services were required. We find also the following advertisement :—

" Dec. 10th, 1798, For Sale 10,000 Lombardy poplars from 10 to 17 feet in height by Wm. Prince, L. I."

The Messrs. Prince from 1819 to 1835 "formed and continued an experimental vineyard," as W.

12*

R. Prince writes me, "comprising four hundred varieties of foreign vineyard grapes, obtained from the Government Nursery of the Luxembourg at Paris; and they collected from every part of our country all the native varieties possible."

Wm. Prince was also engaged in the "silk culture." His cocoonery, (the building is still so called) was situated in the rear of Peck & Fairweather's store, and "yielded large quantities of cocoons, and he planned a filature which was highly successful." He had gloves and stockings woven from his own silk at the manufactory in Philadelphia.

The Garden and Nursery is still conducted by Wm. R. Prince & Co.—the grounds comprising "one hundred and thirteen acres, of which sixty are within the corporate limits of the village."

*Bloodgood Nursery*—Was established by James Bloodgood, in the year 1798. The hands employed vary from twelve to thirty, not as many being employed in winter and mid-summer as in the spring and early summer and autumn.

The proprietors at this time are Joseph Harris King and George B. and Horace Ripley, under the firm of King & Ripley.

*Commercial Garden and Nursery* of Parsons & Co. was commenced in 1838. It comprises about ninety-five acres, and at certain seasons employs over sixty men. Its green-houses, graperies, and entire arrangements are very complete, and well worthy of a visit from every connoisseur in horticultural pursuits. Part of the grounds on which this nursery is located has been in that family for five generations.

*Higgins' Nursery*—Daniel Higgins proprietor, was established in 1836. It covers forty acres and employs from ten to fifty hands.

*Kimber's Nursery*—George D. Kimber proprietor, was commenced in the Fall of 1853; covers ten acres; employs from three to twelve men, and is devoted chiefly to the leading varieties of fruit and ornamental trees, shrubs, vines, etc.

*Silliman's Nursery*—Is located at Bay Side, and covers about six acres. Proprietor, Justice A. G. Silliman.

*Seed Business.*—Formerly the Shakers possessed an almost entire monopoly of this business. Garret R. Garretson was the first to break into this exclusiveness. About sixteen years ago he sent out as an experiment fifty boxes of seeds. He now cultivates about fifty acres, and sends out over three thousand boxes annually. His business extends over our whole country.

*Newspapers.*—The first paper printed in Flushing was called "the Repository," a royal octavo, edited by the students of St. Thomas' Hall. It was commenced in the winter of 1840 and continued about a year and a half. Cotemporaneous with this was "the Church Record," edited by Dr. Hawks; Charles R. Lincoln, Publisher and Printer. It was an Episcopal paper, a quarto, handsomely printed, issued with a cover, and lived about two years.

*Flushing Journal.*—Charles R. Lincoln, Editor and Proprietor. The first number was issued as a specimen sheet in October, 1842. Its regular publication was commenced in March, 1843. It still continues its prosperous course. It has always been the unflinching advocate of improvement and progress in village matters, giving fearless expression to the views of its editor.

*The Public Voice*—Was commenced in 1853, and continued about a year and a half. G. W. Ralph Editor and Proprietor.

*The Long Island Times*—Was established February, 1855. Walter R. Burling, Editor and Proprietor. It still continues its onward way— having the "largest circulation of any paper on the Island outside of the city of Brooklyn."

*Sanford Hall*—Is located on Jamaica Avenue, near the northern limit of the village. The buildings were erected in 1836, by Hon. Nathan Sanford, (generally known as Chancellor Sanford) at

an expense of nearly $130,000. Mr. Sanford
intended the place for his private residence,
but died shortly after its completion, and the
house stood for several years vacant. In the fall
of 1844, Dr. James Macdonald and his brother
Gen. Allan Macdonald purchased the property.
At that time Dr. Macdonald and his brother were
the proprietors of a private institution for the treatment of nervous diseases, located on Murray Hill,
in the city of New York.

In May 1845 they removed their patients to
Sanford Hall, which was then opened as a private
asylum.

In May 1849, Dr. Macdonald* died, and the
establishment has since been conducted by Gen.

---

\* The professional eminence of Dr. Macdonald, his enthusiastic
benevolence, and the exalted purity of his private character, entitle
him to a more extended notice than a mere historical mention. He
was born in Westchester County, New York, in 1803. He was the
youngest son of Dr. Archibald Macdonald, a native of Scotland, who
came to this country in his childhood, and served as Surgeon in the
British Army during the Revolution. In 1824 James graduated from
the College of Physicians and Surgeons, in the City of New York.
Having determined to devote himself to the practice of mental disease
as a specialty, he applied for and obtained the office of Resident Physician of Bloomingdale Asylum. In 1831, having resigned this office,
he was commissioned by the Governors of the New-York Hospital, to
visit the European Asylums, and report improvements, with a view to
their introduction at Bloomingdale. He spent sixteen months in
visiting the various Institutions of England, France, Germany and
Italy. On his return he was invited to take charge of Bloomingdale

A. Macdonald and the widow of his late brother employing the services of a Resident and Consulting Physician.

This institution enjoys a most enviable reputation both at home and abroad. Patients are sent hither from all parts of the Union, and also from the West Indies. Average number under treatment in 1860, forty-eight.

Resident Physician from 1849 to 1854, Dr. Henry W. Buel, now proprietor of Spring Hill Private Asylum, Litchfield, Connecticut. From 1854 to present time, Dr. J. W. Barstow.

Consulting Physician, Benjamin Ogden M. D. New York City.

---

Asylum as Resident Physician and Superintendant. Here he remained until 1837. In 1839, he made a second visit to Europe. In 1841 he opened, in connection with his brother, the Asylum on Murray Hill. In 1845, as above stated, the Institution was removed to Flushing. On May 5th 1849 in the prime of his mature manhood, and in the height of his usefulness, Dr. Macdonald, by a most mysterious Providence, after three days illness, was removed by death; leaving a widow and six children. His disease was pleuro-pneumonia. His funeral took place on May 8th from St. George's Church, of which he had been a vestryman. The shops in the village were closed, and it was a day of sincere and general mourning. Rev. Dr. Ogilbie of New York, preached the funeral sermon from the words "mark the perfect man, and behold the upright; for the end of that man is peace." Thus passed away from earth, one of God's noblest men, beloved in life and lamented in death by all who knew him.

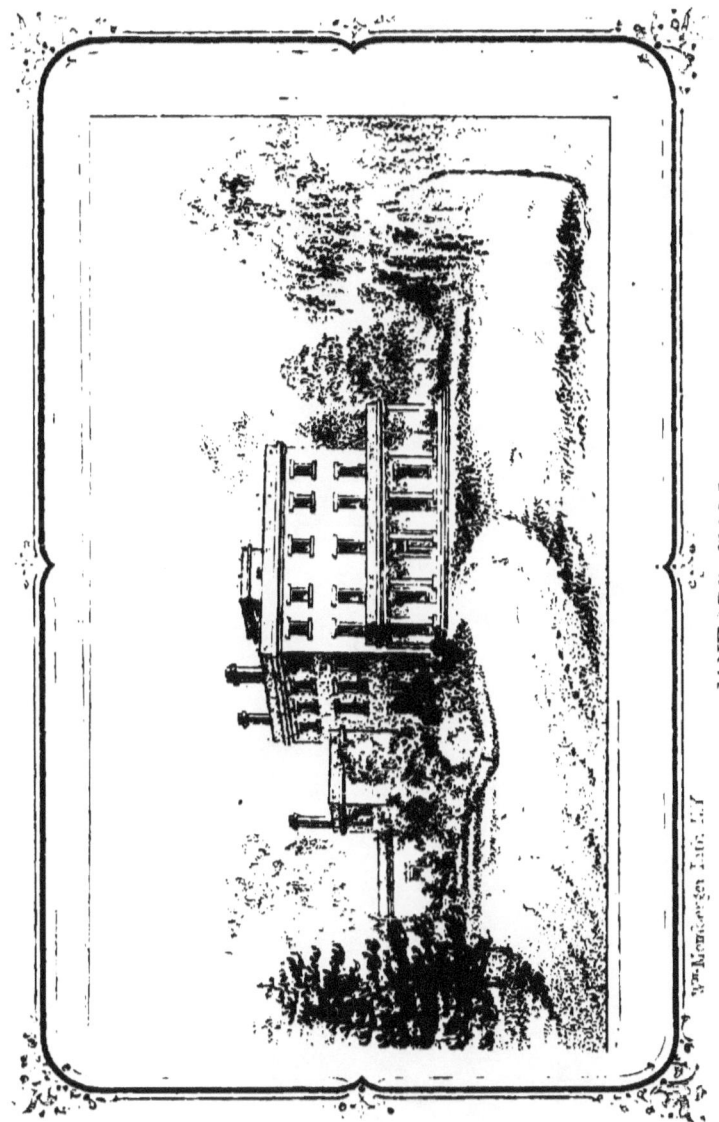

SANFORD HALL.

Wm. Mackenzie Lith. N.Y.

# CHAPTER IX.

RELIGIOUS DENOMINATIONS--SABBATH SCHOOLS, &c.

What ecclesiastical relations the early settlers of the town sustained is not certainly known. They were, however, in all probability, Independents, not connected with the Church of England. For most of the early English emigrants were ; and their first preacher, Mr. Doughty, with his views of the ordinance of baptism, would hardly have been retained within the bosom of the established church.

*Society of Friends.*—In what year this was organized cannot be ascertained with certainty; but it was probably between 1665 and 1669. Previous to the building of the Bowne house, in 1661, we have statements of meetings held in the woods. After its erection they worshipped in it for nearly forty years. The tenets of George Fox were adopted by very many, and Flushing was for many years a strong hold of this society. Its first Yearly Meetings in this country were held here. In the early part of the last century its members were so numerous and able that they could provide, not only for their own necessities, but also for their less favored brethren. In New York city the Friends were so few and feeble that they were unable to furnish themselves with a meeting-house, accordingly the Flushing Friends framed one here, shipped it to New York in a sloop, and had it erected in Green street, a small street extending from Maiden Lane to Liberty street, on the site where subsequently was Grant Thorburn's seed store.

The following interesting article appeared in the New York Observer in connection with this subject. The building sent from Flushing was taken down about the time of the Revolution, and a school-house erected on the site. The Friends owned one hundred feet on Liberty street, and on this was erected a substantial brick building to which reference is had :—

" THE FRIENDS' MEETING-HOUSE."

" *Mr. Printer:*—In the Observer of 20th April last, I remarked, that during the last sixty-four years, in all my doubts, trials, and straits,—not knowing whither to return, to the right hand or to the left, on doing as directed in Proverbs iii. 6, I soon found written on the guide posts, " This is the way; walk ye in it." The following is a case in point :—

In 1824, the Friends' Meeting-house and burying ground stood on the corner of Little Green and

Liberty streets, fronting on Liberty street nearly
one hundred feet, filling all the space to the rear
of the lots fronting on Broadway, and to the rear
of the lots fronting on Maiden Lane. All the families, with one exception, had removed to the upper
part of the city, where several new meeting-houses
were erected, and this one in Liberty street had
been shut up nearly two years. The society resolved to sell the premises at private sale. Before
the matter became public, I waited on certain of
the Friends and was kindly received. I told them
I would not remove a stone from the building, nor
a shovel full of earth from the ground,—that I
would make a seed store in the building, and gar-
nish the sepulchre of their fathers with the roses
of Sharon and the lily of the valley.

They had not yet fixed on the price. Many of
the members were loath to see the meeting-house
demolished, but when they heard of my proposi-
tion, and the use I intended, they gave a willing
consent, Sept. 25, 1824.

I now sat down to consider the aspect of Providence in the matter, Psalms 107, verse 43. 1st.
Being a private sale, and a fixed price, there was
no competition; had it been a public sale it would
have gone beyond my reach. 2d. From the first
conversation on the subject with one of the committee, and on every occasion when I called in fur-

13

therance of my object, I found my man at home, and did the business I intended to my satisfaction. I therefore looked on it as a step which the Lord would bless. On the 27th of September I met one of the committee in Wall street, who said they had concluded to sell, price twenty-five thousand dollars; immediate possession to be given of the meeting-house; the money to be paid on the 1st of May ensuing, when the deed would be given with full possession. Here was another bright spot in my path, which was growing brighter every day. I had all winter to fix the meeting-house for the spring business, and seven months to gather the money.

Isaac Wright called next morning, and asked me to meet the committee in his office at 2 P. M., stating the terms as above.

Hitherto I had kept the matter in my heart: now I consulted my friends. Every one of them said the price was double its worth, and I would be ruined for certain. We dined at half past twelve. I laid the matter before my family—three of my children were of age. My wife and all of them said I would be ruined. I stated my reasons for believing that it was a field which the Lord would bless. They could not see as I did.

I was in the office ten minutes before two. The members of the committee were all there before me. "Friend Grant," said Isaac, "if we sell thee the premises, will thee be able to fulfil the contract on the 1st of May?" Says I, "if alive and well, to-morrow I'll pay you one thousand dollars, and take a receipt part payment. If I don't fulfil my contract on the 1st of May, the $1,000 will be the forfeit." "All fair!" was the response. I paid the $1,000 next day, which clinched the bargain.

Next day the whole city was moved. Grant had bought the meeting-house for $25,000,—double what it was worth,—contrary to the advice of his friends and family; he was a stiff-necked Scottish copperhead, and would be ruined to all intents and purposes.

In two days I was offered *Ten*, and before a month expired I was offered *Twenty Thousand Dollars* for my bargain.

I was now dubbed a *canny* Scotsman, who could see as far through a brick-bat as any hair-splitter or note-shaver in Wall street.

In 1834 I sold the premises for one hundred and five thousand dollars.

GRANT THORBURN, Sen.

*New Haven, June 5th,* 1858."

In 1827 occurred the separation of the Society,—the two branches being subsequently known as the Orthodox and Hicksite Friends. The latter retained possession of the old building. The

Orthodox shortly after occupied another house of worship just east of the old one, which in 1854 gave place to the neat building in which they now worship.

We give copies of a couple of papers from the Bowne collection, connected with the early history of the Friends, evidencing their watchful care over their members and their regard for church government. They may be interesting to those unaccustomed to read communications of this nature in those early times :—

" *From our Monthly Meeting of Women Friends at Philadelphia, 29th 8th mo.* 1708,

*To the Monthly Meeting of Women Friends at Flushing, L. I.—Greeting :*

Dear Friends,—

To you is the Salutation of Love in our Lord Jesus Christ desiring your prosperity and Welfare in the unchangeable Truth. And these may allso further certify you that Request was made to this meeting in the Behalfe of our friend Mary Guest for a Certificate and according to the Good order established amongst us due Inquiry hath been made and we doe not find but that She hath been of a Sober and Honest Conversation and that she may witness a Growth and Prosperity in the truth of which she hath made profession is the desire of our Souls so Committing her to your

Care we remain your friends and sisters in the near relation and fellowship of the Gospel of Peace. Signed in the behalfe of our said Meeting by

SARAH GOODSON" and others.

" *From Our Yearly Meeting held at Philadelphia for Pennsylvania and New Jersey from the 20th to the 24th day of Seventh month inclusive 1735, To the next Yearly Meeting to be held in Flushing on Long Island.*

Dearly Beloved Friends,—

In the fellowship of the Gospel of our Christ our Head and High Priest we tenderly Salute you, desiring that you and wee and his Gathered Churches as well as particular Members every where may walk werthy of the Manifold and Repeated blessings which he mercifully vouchsafes unto his people, amongst which the visitation and attendance of his Living Presence in our assemblys Calls for our Particular and grateful acknowlegement, as well as a Suitable Circumspection in Conversation and Zeal for the promotion of His Glorious Truth in the Earth to the Honour of his Great and worthy name. Such a Perseverance would infallibly draw down and continue the Divine and Heavenly Blessing upon the Churches. And now dear Friends wee hereby acquaint you that this our Anniversary Meeting was large and Comfurtable wherein many living Testimonys

13*

were born and our Lord according to His Promise
to those that should meet in his name was with
us to the great encouragement and consolation of
the faithfull, begetting in them fresh resolutions
to go in the way that is cast up for the Ransom-
ed to walk in, and such will be as Lights in the
world and Good Examples to the youth or others
who take undue Liberty's and we know that Example goes before Precept. By the accounts from
our several Quarterly Meetings it appears that
Love and unity is generally maintained amongst
Friends and the Discipline in a good Degree put
into practice; the affairs of the Church were
transacted in Peace and Condecsension according
to the Apostles Advice. Wee received your Last
yearly meeting Epistle and were glad to under-
stand you had a comfortable meeting and now wee
conclude remaining your friends and Brethren in
the unity and Fellowship of a blessed Truth.

Signed by order and on behalf of our said meeting by                         JOHN KIMLEY, *Clerk*."

Of the preachers we can of course give no connected history. They left no record of Seminary
Diplomas; of ordination by laying on of hands,
either by Bishop or Presbytery; of call, settlement and departure. Their commission to pro-
claim the Gospel of Truth, they claimed, was obtained immediately from the great Bishop and

Head, without the human intervention of ecclesiastical courts. Their qualifications for their
work were imparted by the Inspiring Spirit, without the help of theological institutions. How
much truth their claims express it is not our province here to discuss.

We give a condensed narrative of an interesting series of events in the history of one of their
preachers, Samuel Bownas. He was an Englishman by birth; a man of considerable note and
preaching power, travelling from place to place,
making religious visits to Friends in this country .
He landed in Maryland " about the 29th of Fifth
month, 1792." Here he met George Keith, of
whom a more full account will shortly be given,
who challanged him to a public dispute in the
following letter :—

" *To the Preacher lately arrived from England.*
Sir,—

I intend to give Notice after Sermon, that
you and myself are to dispute To-morrow, and
would have you give Notice thereof accordingly.

Sir, I am your humble Servant,

GEORGE KEITH.

*Dated the* 1*st Sunday in August,* 1702."

To this the following reply was sent :—
" George Keith,--

I Have received thine, and think myself no way

obliged to take any Notice of one that hath been
so very mutable in his Pretences to Religion ; besides, as thou hast long since been disowned, after
due Admonition given thee by our Yearly-Meeting
in London, for thy quarrelsome and irregular Prac-
tices, thou art not worthy of my Notice, being no
more to me than a Heathen Man and a Publican ;
is the needful from

SAMUEL BOWNAS."

Dated same day.

He prosecuted his journey until he reached Long
Island.  G. Keith followed and appointed meetings in the same places with himself, and was considered the chief instigator of the persecution to
which he was subjected.  On the 29th of Nov.
1702, he was present at half-yearly meeting at
Flushing, which was very largely attended.
" When the Meeting was fully set," he says, " the
High-Sheriff came with a very large Company
with him, who were all armed ; some had Guns,
others Pitchforks, others Swords, Clubs, Halberts,
&c., as if they should meet with great opposition
in taking a poor silly harmless Sheep out of the
Flock."  Stepping up to him the Sheriff took him
by the hand, saying, "You are my Prisoner." "By
what authority ?"  He showed his warrant to arrest Samuel Bowne.  "That is not my name.
That Friend's name is so." "We know him ;

that's not the man, but you are the man : pray then, what's your name?" "That is a question that requires consideration, whether proper to answer or not." At length the officer and his retinue were invited to remain till the services were ended ; which they did, depositing their arms outside the building. Bownas, "finding the Word like as a fire," preached with more than his usual power. After meeting an arrangement was made with the Sheriff, by which he remained from Saturday until the next Thursday. On Wednesday there was a funeral of an influential Quaker, which was attended by nearly two thousand people. He then went to Hempstead. The court required him to give bail in two thousand pounds,—himself in one thousand pounds, and two Friends in five hundred pounds each. This he refused, saying, "if as small a sum as *three half pence* would do, I should not do it." He was accordingly committed to "the common goal." On the 28th of Dec. court met; his case was submitted to the Grand Jury, who returned the bill "indorsed ignoramus." The presiding Judge was exceedingly angry, and uttered severe threats against the Jury; to which he was appropriately answered by James Clement, one of their number. At length they again retired to deliberate and the next day returned the same answer. Upon which they were dismissed, and the prisoner remanded into custody. He was refused a copy of the indictment against him. He was by trade a blacksmith, but this he could not pursue within his prison-bars. Preferring to earn his support, to receiving it from the liberality of Friends, he learned the trade of a shoemaker, through the kindness of one Charles Williams, a Scotch churchman, who pursued that business near by. He soon became so skilful that he could earn fifteen shillings a week. During his imprisonment he was visited by an Indian King and three Chiefs, with whom he held a long conversation. At length, Sept. 2d, 1703, court again assembled, and his case was presented to another Grand Jury, who in a short time returned the papers endorsed " ignoramus ;" " which gave some of the Lawyers cause to say, in a jocular way, they were got into an *Ignoramus Country*." On the next day he was set at liberty by proclamation, " and a large Body of dear Friends had me with them in a kind of Triumph." He had been in jail over eleven months. Henceforth he gave up shoemaking and resumed his old business of preaching, visiting the Island and other portions of the country, and reached England in October, 1706.

*Protesant Episcopal Church.*—Rev. George Keith, of whom previous mention has been made was born at Aberdeen, Scotland. He was not of Quaker parentage. In what year he joined the society of Friends is not known. He was a man of learning. His talents were of a high order. His mind was acute and logical. His temper was fearless and unyielding. Hence, what he undertook he prosecuted with unflagging zeal ; his feelings often carrying him far beyond the limits of christian courtesy and charity. He first appeared in this country in East Jersey, in 1682. He was then a Quaker, and held the office of Surveyor General. In 1689 he removed to Philadelphia as tutor to the children of some wealthy families, " at the same time exercising his preaching faculty." In 1691 he began to dispute with the Quakers, and finally separated from them after being a preacher among them twenty-eight years. In 1694 he went to England and was admitted to orders in the established Church. In April, 1702, he sailed for America. In August, 1704, he again arrived in England and became Rector of Edburton, in Sussex, where he died.

It was while on his visit to America that he visited Flushing. He came as a missionary, appointed by " the Society for the propagation of the Gospel in Foreign Parts." He first attempted to deliver his message in Flushing, to Friends when assembled for their worship. But, because

of his apostacy from their society, his determined
opposition to them, and his supposed, if not known
instigation of persecution against their preacher,
Bownas, he was met by a very decided resistance
and was not allowed to deliver his message.
On his first visit he was accompained by Rev. Mr.
Vesey of New York, Rev. John Talbot, and several Episcopal gentlemen from Jamaica. He
says, " After some time of silence I began to
speak, standing up in the gallery where their
speakers use to stand when they speak; but I
was so much interrupted by the Clamour and
Noise, that several of the Quakers made, forbidding me to speak, that I could not proceed." Then
a Friend followed with an address " about an
hour." Then ensued a discussion · in which he
was charged with defrauding the poor of fifty
pounds, which he denied with indignation. "Dec.
3d, 1702. I visited again the Quaker meeting at
Flushing, Long Island, having obtained a letter
from Lord Cornbury, to two Justices of Peace
to go along with me, to see that the Quakers
should not interrupt me as they had formerly
done. But notwithstanding the two Justices that
came along with me to signifie my Lord Cornbury's Mind, by his Letter to them, which was read
to them in their Meeting by Mr. Talbot, they used
the like interruption as formerly, and took no no-

tice of my Lord Cornbury's Letter, more than if
it had been from any private person." But his
efforts were unsuccessful. He was in all probability the first Episcopal minister who attempted
to perform the service of that church in Flushing. In what year the present church was organized cannot be determined. In a report by
Rev. Mr. Vesey, to the Society at home, dated
Oct 5th, 1704, he says, at "Flushing there is no
Church." It "is inhabited by Quakers." Rev.
Mr. Urquhart of Jamaica "Preaches on the third
Sunday, and prays twice at Newtown and Flushing once a month on the week days, and by the
blessing of God, the Congregations in the respective towns daily increase."

C. Congreve in a report to the society, in 1704,
says, "Flushing is another Town in the same
County, most of the inhabitants thereof are Quakers, who rove through the Country from one village to another, talk Blasphemy, Corrupt the
Youth, and do much mischief."

Rev. James Honyman, in a letter to the society,
of April 15th, 1704, says, "Newtown and Flushing famous for being stocked with Quakers, whither
I intend to go upon their meeting-days on purpose to preach Lectures against their errors."
Whether he carried his charitable "purpose" into

14

execution is not known, as he continued at Jamaica but a short time.

In 1705, Rev. W. Urquhart was settled at Jamaica, bestowing part of his time upon Flushing and Newtown. Of him John Talbot writes, " Mr. U. is well chosen for the people of Jamaica, and indeed I think none fitter than the Scotch Episcopal to deal with Whigs and Fanaticks of all sorts."

July 18th, 1710, Rev. Thomas Poyer was inducted into the church at Jamaica. When he arrived the dissenters had possession of the church and parsonage. The latter they retained, but the former Mr. Poyer soon preached in again. A brief account of the works of this early laborer in this field may properly be inserted in this place. He entered the service of the society, September 29th, 1709. He embarked for America October 31st, but owing to various delays the ship did not sail until April 10th following. Meanwhile his wife had been twice delayed by sickness, and it was necessary to take her ashore to secure the services of a Physician. Their voyage lasted from April 10th to July 7th. On that day they were shipwrecked on Long Island, about one hundred miles from Jamaica, to which place he was appointed. His parish, he writes, " is fifteen miles long and six and a half broad," and his salary thirty-nine pounds sterling. This was paid to the Presbyterian minister. Tedious and expensive law-suits resulted. His hands were filled with work and his heart with sorrows. He was reduced to circumstances of extreme necessity. He writes to the society that "their poor missionary is laboring under many difficulties, and reduced to the want of a great many necessaries; two Gowns and Cassocks I have already worn out in their service, a third is worn very bare and my family wants are so many and pressing that I know not how I shall procure another." Upon this the society presented him with a gown and cassock and ten pounds "in money or goods as he preferred." Again he writes, " now to do this and to visit my people which I am often obliged to who live distant from me many of them about twelve miles I am necessitated to keep two horses which is very expensive and troublesome to me and consumes me more Clothes in one year than would serve another who is not obliged to ride for three or four. In Newtown and Flushing for want of the convenience of private houses I am forced to make use of Public ones which is a very great charge to me for I bring some of my family generally with me. If I did not they would be one-half of the year without opportunities of Public Worship." Again, " Our poor Church has been in great distress ever since I came here, and myself, the unworthy Minister of it threatened to be starved and denied victuals for my money, and my corn sent me home from the Mill with this message from the Miller, 'I might eat it whole as the hogs do, he would not grind for me'" —that the people threatened if the Constables attempted to collect the assessment for the Salary, "they will scald them; they will stone them; they will go to Club-law with them, and I know not what." Again, after stating his arrearages in salary: " & a great deal of sickness I had myself & and in my family all of us being seldom in health at the name time, I have buried two wives & two children in less than five years and am now eleven in family the eldest of my family being little more than 16 years of age, there is the expense of every other Sunday when I go to Newtown & Flushing to be borne for myself and those of the children I take with me, then all other necessaries to be bought, £16 to be paid yearly for house rent & all this to come out of my stipend, no one of them (his children) being able to get & indeed too young to know how to save what is gotten; this my Lord is too great burthen upon me." Finally the church itself by suit at law is taken from them, and he writes, "tho' I have endeavoured as patiently as I could

to bear up under all these trials besides the loss of
two wives & several children yet the infirmities
of old age bear very hard upon me insomuch that
I feel myself almost unable to officiate at the three
churches of Jamaica, Newtown and Flushing as
I have hitherto done and which is absolutely necessary for the Minister of the Parish to do."
He then requests permission to leave his mission
and return to England. Against this a Rev. Mr.
Campbell protests, in a letter to the Society, in
which he says, Mr. Poyer " is a grandson of Coll.
Poyer who died in the gallant defence of Pem-
broke Castle in the time of Oliver Cromwell ;
that he is a good natured honest man and is bene-
ficent to his neighbors," and that his recall " would
infallibly ruin the poor Gentleman and his numerous family."

At length it pleased the Great Master to call
his tried and afflicted servant to his rest and re-
ward. He died January 15th, 1731, (O. S )

Rev. Mr. Thomas, of Hempstead, in writing to
the Society of the troubles in Jamaica, concludes
with the following flourish :—" All the rest of the
Missionaries are settled in peace, and if these
people are nipped in the bud and Mr. Poyer restored to his right, I presume they will scarce
offer to flutter again as long as there is a crowned
head that sways the Sceptre of Great Britain."

14*

Rev. Thomas Colgan succeeded. In 1735 he writes, " Several of the Quakers of Flushing do as often as it is my turn to officiate there attend upon Divine Service. This it is that opens a clear *prospectus* for the conversion of many souls which God in his own time will make to the true Church of Christ." Sept. 29th, 1744, " The several Churches belonging to my cure (Jamaica, Newtown and Flushing) are in a very peaceable and growing state." Sept. 29th, 1746, " In my letter of the 26th March last I gave information to the Society of our being in a very likely way of having a Church erected in the town of Flushing." Previous to this they had worshipped in the Old Guard House. He then requests the Society to " bestow upon it a Bible & Common Prayer Book according to their usual bounty for certainly there can be no set of People within this Province who are greater objects of the Society's pity and charity than those belonging to the town of Flushing of which I have been so truly Sensible that it has brought me (if I may be permitted thus to express it) to double my diligence in that place where error & impiety greatly abound." From this it appears the first church edifice was erected in 1746. It was a small building with a spire. The ground was donated by Capt. Hugh Wentworth, who had his country seat on what is now known as the Redwood property. It stood just north of the present building in the same yard. The expense of the spire was defrayed by Messrs. John Aspinwall and Thomas Grennall. Mr. Aspinwall also presented the church with "a very fine bell of about five hundred weight." This same bell rang its notes for nearly a century when its materials were recast and incorporated in the present one. The old chancel rail, the old Bible given by the society, and the prayer books used in the church, the oldest bearing date 1746, are now in possession of the Rector. The number of communicants at that time was about twenty. So that the church must have been organized some time previously, but when or by whom there is no record.

March 28th, 1749, Colgan writes :—" I have great hopes that our Church at Flushing will in a little time gain ground among the Quakers who are very numerous there, and it is somewhat remarkable and may be thought worty of notice, that a man who had for many years strictly adhered to the principles of Quakerism, when that new church was opened and a collection made he gave money for the use of that church, but thinking he had not put enough in the Plate, went immediately after service and gave more to the

Collector." A thousand pities he had not told his name, that such an example of liberality in sentiment and purse might have been perpetuated for the benefit of succeeding generations.

Mr. Colgan died in 1753, and was succeeded in 1757 by Rev. Samuel Seabury. Oct. 10th, 1759, he writes, "Flushing in the last generation the ground seat of Quakerism is in this the Seat of Infidelity." In 1761, a Mr. Tredwell, a graduate of Yale College, acted as lay reader to the church. In this year also the charter of incorporation, by the name and style of "St. George's Church," was granted by Lieut. Gov. Colden. In what year Seabury died we do not know. But after his death "a handsome house" was built and presented to his widow.

Feb. 17th, 1770. Rev. Joshua Bloomer writes, "I preach at the three churches of Jamaica, Newtown and Flushing alternately, and generally to crowded assemblies, who behave during divine service with the utmost decency and decorum, the churches are neat, well finished buildings. But those of Newton and Flushing rather small for the Congregations."

April 9th, 1777. On account of political troubles "my church was shut up for five Sundays when the King's troops landed whose success has restored us to those religious principles of which we were deprived by tyranny and persecution."

The church at Flushing was subsequently enlarged, but in what year is not known.

For much of what follows we are indebted to Rev. J. C. Smith.

1795. Much discussion existed between the vestry of Jamaica and those of Newtown and Flushing, relating to the arrangement of services. The unhappy controversy waxed warm, and the old chronicler pathetically observes, " the church wardens and vestry of Newtown and Flushing went off in a very abrupt manner and left the church wardens and vestry of Jamaica to themselves." A separation was demanded, but did not then take place.

1797, January 15th. Jamaica called a minister, but the other churches did not unite.

1797, May 10th. Flushing called Rev. E. D. Rattoone, in which Jamaica united but Newtown withdrew from the union. Rev. Mr. Rattoone resided midway between Flushing and Jamaica. He was to preach in Flushing every other sabbath in winter and every sabbath afternoon during the remainder of the year. His salary per annum was the interest of nine hundred pounds, and one hundred pounds additional were pledged, *if it could be raised!* He presented the present corporate seal to the church, though by vote of the vestry he was subsequently reimbursed for it, and blank-books amounting to four pounds and four shillings.

Oliver Bowne was sexton on a salary of six pounds per annum and the privilege of *cutting the grass in the church yard*. The clerk was allowed the same sum, but instead of grass extra was to receive an admonition for past irregular conduct.

1800. There appears this very singular and anomolous statement in ecclesiastical history, "both churches experienced a want of funds."

1802. As a consequence of this deficiency in the treasury Flushing and Jamaica again disagreed. The former complained that the latter obtained subscriptions from her members and resolved to withdraw if not discontinued. This threat weighed very seriously with the Jamaica brethren, who sagaciously resolved that "it would not be for the advantage of *this* church to support a clergyman separately," and determined to discountenance the solicitations. Meanwhile Mr. Rattoone resigned and removed, and left the belligerents to fight their own battles. Flushing was not pacified with the pacific submission of Jamaica, and resolved to separate. Communications were opened with Newtown, and an agreement to unite was effected.

1803, April 20th.   Newtown and Flushing called Rev. Abm. L. Clark.

1809, October 3d.   Mr. C. confined his services to the former and the church at Flushing became vacant.

1809, November 4th, Rev. Brazilla Buckley was called, sole Rector of St. George's Church, who remained until his death, March 9, 1820.

1820, August 7th, Rev. J. V. E. Thorne was called, and it was " Resolved, that a new church be erected." Thomas Philips, James Bloodgood and Isaac Peck were appointed a building committee.   It was consecrated to the service of God May 25th, 1821.

1826.  Rev. W. A. Muhlenberg, D. D. was called.

1829, Feb. 5th, Rev. W. H. Lewis, D. D. was called.

1833, Sept. 3d,   "    J. M. Forbes was called.

1834,   "   6th,  "    S. R. Johnson was called.

1835, Oct. 20th,  "    R. B. Van Kleek was called.

1837, Dec. 6th,   "    Fred. Goodwin was called.

1838.  The church edifice was enlarged at a cost of seventeen hundred dollars, and twenty-six new pews added.

1844, in March, Rev. George Burcher was called. He died in May, 1847, and in

1847, Nov. Rev. J. Carpenter Smith, the present
Rector, entered upon his duties.

1853, May 18th, the corner stone of the present
edifice was laid with the customary ceremonies.
The building was consecrated in June, 1854. In
the meantime the old building was removed
to its present site, and during 1858 was rejuve-
nated, and is now used for a sunday school and
lecture room.

· The new building cost, including fixtures, thir-
ty-three thousand dollars. Isaac Peck, Allan
Macdonald and Wm. H. Schemerhorn were the
building committee.

Zion Church at Little Neck. This was erect-
ed in 1830, by Alderman Wynant Van Zandt. Its
Rectors have been Revd. Messrs. Eli Wheeler,
Ralph Williston, Christian F. Cruse, and Henry
M. Beane, the present incumbent, who was settled
in May, 1842.

Grace Church at Whitestone. This building
was erected by Samuel Leggett, a member of the
society of Friends, for the use of all religious denominations, with the hope of bringing about a
reformation in the neighborhood. Services were
conducted from time to time by Rectors of the
Episcopal Church at Flushing. In 1855 the building was rented from the executors of Mr. Leggett,

and Rev. Wm. Short was called by the vestry of St. George's Church, and commenced regular service in July of that year. The connection with the old parish was dissolved September 6th, 1858, and Rev. Wm. Short was chosen Rector by the wardens and vestrymen. The congregation contemplate the erection of a new edifice, to be built of brick, in Gothic style, and to cost 6,000 dollars.

The first officers were Ab'm B. Sands, John D. Locke, Wardens; A. H. Kissam, Henry Lowerree, Henry Smith, Peter F. Westervelt, Griffith Rowe, Charles H. Miller, Ab'm Binninger and John Barrow, Vestrymen.

*Protestant Methodist Episcopal Church.*—The first Methodist church in the village was the African Macedonian church in Liberty street. It was organized in 1811. This edifice was rebuilt in 1837. Rev. Benjamin Griffin, a white preacher, in his circuit officiated for them. At that time there was not a single white family of Methodists in the place, so that this self-denying brother was accommodated with food and lodgings by his colored brethren.

Rev Samuel Cockrance was the first Methodist minister that preached in Flushing to a white congregation. His audience numbered about twelve persons. The meeting was held in a house adjoining Garretson's seed store, in Liberty street.

His text was " fear not, little flock ; for it is your
Father's good pleasure to give you the kingdom."
They afterwards worshipped in two different pla-
ces in Main street. In

1822 they purchased lots in Washington street,
and erected the building in which they worshipped until

1843, when they entered into their present edifice
in Main street. In

1859 they repaired their building, erected a tower,
purchased an organ, and made other improvements, at a cost of 3,500 dollars.

1824, August 14th, Flushing Circuit was organized. The following is the list of preachers
in their church :—

1824, Revds. John Luckey and J. W. Le Fever,
1825,   "     Robert Seeny and Luman Andrews.
1826,   "     Richard Seaman and B. Creagh.
1827,   "     "     " and O. V. Amerman.
1828—9,  Rev.  Ira Ferris,
1830—1,   "    Joseph D. Marshall,
1832—3,   "    Charles F. Pelton,
1834,     "    Alexander Hulin,
1835,     "    David Plumb,
1836,     "    John L. Gilder,
1837—8,   "    William Thatcher,
1839,     "    Daniel Wright,
1840,     "    George Brown,

| 1841, | Rev. | Elbert Osborn, |
| 1842, | " | John J. Matthias, |
| 1843—4, | " | Benjamin Griffin, |
| 1845—6, | " | David Osborn, |
| 1847, | " | John W. B. Wood, |
| 1848—9, | " | John B. Merwin, |
| 1850, | " | Samuel W. Law, |
| 1851, | " | Abra'm S. Francis, |
| 1852—3, | " | Ira Abbott, |
| 1854—5, | " | William F. Collins, |
| 1856—7, | " | Thomas H. Burch, |
| 1858, | " | J. L. Peck, |
| 1860, | " | R. M. Hatfield, |

There is also a Methodist church in Whitestone, which was organized March 28th, 1850. The edifice was erected the same year at a cost of twelve hundred dollars. In 1853 the basement was finished, costing three hundred dollars. In 1852 Rev. A. Van Rensalear Abbott was appointed Pastor. In 1855 Rev. Richard Wake was appointed, and remained one year. For two years subsequently Rev. Mr. Fitch, then Principal of the Public School at Flushing, preached on Sabbath evenings, and Orange Judd had charge of the Sabbath school. In 1858 Rev. David Tuthill was appointed Pastor, remaining nine months and then leaving as Missionary to Arizona. In 1859 Rev. D. A. Goodsell, the present Pastor, was appointed.

*Protestant Reformed Dutch Church.*—Rev. William R. Gordon commenced to preach here while still settled at Manhasset as Pastor. The meetings were first held in a hall in Bridge street; afterwards in a school house in Church street. The church was organized in 1842, with six members. The church edifice was erected in 1844. It cost about twelve thousand dollars. The building committee were Gardiner G. Howland and William Henry Roe. The stone came from Blackwell's Island. In 1850 Mr. Gordon resigned and removed to New York. After an interval of nearly eighteen months, the Rev. G. Henry Mandeville was called July 28th, 1851. In the spring of 1859 the church was enlarged and repaired, and an organ purchased at an expense of about three thousand dollars. In August of this year Rev. Mr. Mandeville removed to Newburg. In September Rev. W. W. Halloway was called and settled as Pastor.

*Congregational Church.*—This church was organized early in the spring of 1851. They first worshipped in a school house in church street. In the fall of 1851, Rev. Charles O. Reynolds was called and settled as Pastor. In 1852 they built at the head of Washington street, in Union street, the Chapel which has since been removed to Ailanthus place. This church edifice was built in 1856,

REFORMED PROTESTANT DUTCH CHURCH

Wm Momberger, Lith NY

at a cost of fourteen thousand dollars. Building committee, D. S. Williams, E. Treadwell, Robert B. Parsons, Edward Roe and W. Phillips.

In December, 1854, Rev. S. Bourne was called, who resigned in the spring of 1859, and was succeeded in Feb. 1860, by Rev. Henry Staats.

*Baptist Church.*—This was organized January 17th, 1857. They held their meetings at first in the school room of the late Jemima Hammond. The present church edifice was built in the spring of 1857, and dedicated October 15th of the same year. Rev. Howard Osgood was the first Pastor. He was succeeded by Rev. Oscar Greaves, who officiated for a few months, and was, followed by the present Pastor, Rev. John Bray. It is a singular circumstance that a church of this denomination should not have existed here at an earlier date; particularly when we remember that the first religious teacher in Flushing entertained their views in relation to the ordinance of Baptism.

*Roman Catholic Church.*—The following statement of this church was kindly furnished by its present Minister :—

St. Michael's Church.—In October, 1826, the Catholics of Flushing, then only twelve in number, invited the Rev. Father Farnham of Brooklyn to come and minister to them the consolations of

15*

their holy religion. Accordingly, their first meeting was held, and the first Mass offered up in a small house on Main street, adjoining the Post Office. It was soon found to be too small, and it was deemed expedient to purchase a larger house in Liberty street, where they were attended regularly once a month by the Rev. Mr. Curran of Astoria. This, too, after being twice enlarged, became insufficient to accommodate the congregation, now rapidly increasing. In order to meet the wants of the people, it became a matter of necessity to purchase a new site, and erect a new church. On the 28th of June, 1841, four lots were purchased on the corner of Union and Madison streets, where the present church now stands, and a frame building seventy-two by thirty-five feet was erected. As soon as it became known that there was a Catholic church in Flushing, the congregation increased amazingly; and application was made to Bishop Hughes for a resident pastor which was immediately acceded to, and the congrgation entrusted to the pastoral charge of the Rev. Mr. Wheeler, who, after a few years was succeeded by the Rev. John McMahon. Again in 1854, the church being found entirely too small to contain the congregation, and in too dilapidated a condition to be enlarged, a meeting was held, and it was unanimously resolved to build a church of larger dimensions and of some architectural pretensions. Accordingly, the present beautiful Gothic structure was erected under the direction and supervision of the Rev. James O'Beirne. present pastor, aided and encouraged by the most hearty and zealous cooperation of the congregation. The corner stone was laid on the 24th of June, 1854, and on the following Christmas Day, the holy sacrifice of the Mass was offered up in the Church, though yet in an unfinished state. Notwithstanding the great exertions of the pastor and people, and the munificent donations of many ladies and gentlemen of different persuasions, it was found impossible for want of funds to complete the work before the end of Sept. 1856. On the 4th of Oct. of the same year it was solemnly dedicated to the service of Almighty God by the Right Rev. Dr. Loughlin, Bishop of Brooklyn.

St. Fidelis Roman Catholic Church at College Point was erected and dedicated in 1856. It is under the pastoral charge of Rev. Joseph Huber, a native of Austria.

The Lutheran Church at College Point.— In the spring of 1857 the Lutheran families of Strattonport established a school and employed Mr. G. Soeler, a candidate for the ministry, as teacher. He also preached for them from time to time. In October, 1857 their present church edifice was completed at a cost of fifteen hundred dollars. In April, 1858 Rev. August Heitmuller was called as Pastor, who also conducted the school. They have no sabbath school. The whole congregation are catechized every sabbath afternoon.

St. Paul's Free Chapel at College Point.—In 1859 the Flushing Bible Society discontinued the services of their colporteur, Mr. Caldwell, who had been faithfully laboring at Strattonport and College Point for two years. With the increase of the population of the village was a corresponding increase in the attendance at the sunday school, which had been held hitherto in the district school house. It was determined to erect a Free Chapel, and Mr. W. O. Chisolm of College Point, and Messrs. F. A. Potts, O. W. Whitney, Spencer H Smith, W. H. Stebbins, Jr. and H. A. Bogert, were appointed a committee to carry out the plan. Mr. Poppenhusen generously donated a plot of ground, and nearly three thousand dollars was raised by subscription in the town. The building was completed January 1st, 1860.

The Mission Chapel at the Head of the Vleigh was erected in 1858, at a cost of upwards of one thousand dollars, a great part of which was generously contributed by a lady of the village, whose many acts of unostentatious charity have caused her name to be often breathed with a blessing at the lonely hearth of the suffering poor, The plot of ground upon which the building stands was donated by Thomas Whitson. A fair in aid of the Chapel, held in 1859, realized five hundred and forty dollars.

*Sabbath Scoools* —The first school held on the Sabbath was for instructing colored people in the elementary branches of education. It was conducted mainly by Friends, assisted by Wm. A. Haughton. This was about 1819—20.

The Sabbath school connected with the Episcopal church was commenced in 1820. Mr. Haughton was its superintendant. He was assisted by Messrs. Richard Peck, Isaac Peck, James Morrell and others, together with a number of ladies.

Messrs. Haughton and Richard Peck also made the first efforts to institute a Sabbath school at Whitestone, at about the same time. They were joined by some of the inhabitants, principally ladies. They labored there about three years, and exerted a very happy influence.

The colored Sunday school in connection with the Episcopal church was commenced about nine years ago. It had its origin in a class taught by a young lady, a member of that church. The class became too large for the room where they met, and was transferred to the Episcopal Sabbath school room.

The school of the Methodist Church was organized about 1823.

The schools of the other churches were organized about cotemporaneously with the churches.

A Mission Sabbath School was commenced at the District School House in College Point in 1855, by members of different religious denominations in the town. It still continues in successful operation at the Mission Chapel recently erected. Sabbath Schools have also been established within a recent period at the Mission Chapel at the Head of the Vleigh, Black Stump, the Alley and Bay Side.

CONCLUSION.—Thus have we presented such facts as we have had opportunity to collect. We might have entered into further details concerning the later period of our history. But our object has been to gather, not so much the late as the early incidents. Of these we think we have obtained all now accessible. We offer it to our fellow-townsmen in the hope that they will be interested in the narrative, imperfect as it necessarily must be. How great changes have transpired since, a little over two centuries ago, our fathers settled in this pleasant and beautiful spot. Then the Indian was " Monarch of all he surveyed" " to the manor native born." Then the wolf and the bear had their favorite haunts in the wild

forests that threw their solemn shadow over all
the land,   What prophetic eye can look down the
vista of the future and discern the changes which
the chronicler two centuries hence will have to
record.

In the review with what pathos and solemnity
does the question appeal to every reflective mind
and sensitive heart, "Our fathers, where are they?"

From this mortal scene,
Gone with the dream of things that were,
  As if they n'er had been,
Beyond the wanderings of the morn,
  Beyond the portals of the day,
Unto a land whence none return,
  Our fathers, where are they ?


The vanished comet, long deemed lost,
  And absent for a thousand years,
Again, amid the starry host,
  From darkness reappears.
Seas ebb and flow upon the shore,
  Moons wax when they have waned away,
But they who go to come no more,
  Our fathers, where are they ?


Thou Sun, that light'st the boundless skies,
  Where are the Earth's departed gone ?
Ye stars, to your all-seeing eyes,
  Is the great secret known?

Ye breathe not of their place of rest,
  But roll in silence on your way,
And the lorn echoes of the breast,
  Still answer where are they?"

"'Tis thus, in future hours, some bard will say,
  Of you who read, and him who sings this lay,
They are gone—they *all* are gone."

Would we leave a record which we would desire future generations to read, then let each one

              "Seek to slay
The rank and fatal errors of the day:
Battle upon the side of truth and right,
War for the good and beautiful—the fight
May be thy last, but it will be thy best,
For every blood-drop on thy brow or breast,
Shall sanctify the issue, and shall be
Transformed to gems, by heaven's strange alchemy,
That shall bedeck thy forehead."

FINIS.

# APPENDIX.

---

*List of heads of Families in Flushing, (French, Dutch and English) from 1645 to 1698, gathered from various old records and documents,* By Henry Onderdonk, Jr.

John Adams; Poulas Amerman; Thomas Applegate; Derick, John and Elbert Areson; Anthony Badgley; Cornelius Barneson; William Benger; Rudolf Blackford; George Blee; John, Elizabeth and Francis Bloodgood; Barnardus Bloom; Samuel, Mary, John and Thomas Bowne; Derick Brewer; Charles Bridges; Moses Brown; Lyman Bumptell; Francis Burto; Widow Cartwright; Wm. Chadderton; Richard Chew; James and John Clement; Rebecca Clery; Nathaniel Coe; Francis Colley; Hugh Cowperthwaite; Adrian, John and Patience Cornelius; Jacob and Richard Cornell; Mindert Corten; William Danford; Thomas Davis; Obadiah Demilt; John Depre; John Dewildie; Lawrence (or Dutch,) Douse; Elias, Sarah, Francis and Charles Doughty; Deborah Ebell; John Embree; John Esmond; Edward, Dorothy, John, Matthew and Thomas Farrington; Edward, James and Tobias Feake; Anthony, Benjamin, John, Thomas, Joseph and Robert Sr. and Jr. Field; Robert Firman; Esther, John and Thomas Ford; William, *weaver*, William, *carpenter*, Fowler; Henry Franklin; John Furman; John Furbosh (or Forbush;) John Genung; John Gelloe (or Gilime;?) Wowter Gilbertson; John Glover; Edward Sr. and Jr., Richard and John Griffin; Lorus Haff; Sam'l Haight; Thomas Hall; Garrit Hanson; Edward Hart; John Harrington; John Harrison; Mr. Matthias Haroye; Benjamin, John and William Haviland; John Heeded; Joseph and Thomas Hedger; Gerrit Hendricks; Thomas, *Justice*, and John Hicks; John, Robert and Thomas Hinchman; Powell Hoff; Dennis Holdren; John Sr. and Jr. Hopper; Samuel Hoyt; Benjamin

Hubbard; Nathan Jeffs; Josiah Jenning; John Jores; Thos. Kimsey; Harmanus King; George Langley; John, Joseph, Thomas, and Major William Lawrence; Madalin Lodew; John Man; John Marston; Michael Millner (or Millard;) Charles Morgan; William and Ann Noble; Phillip Odall; William Owen; Elias and Joseph Palmer; Nicholas Parcell (or Persells;) Daniel Patrick; Mary Perkins; Wm. Pidgeon; Derick Poules; Arthur Powel; Edward Rause (or Reurt;) Abm. Rich; John Rodman; David and Nathaniel Rowe; Thomas Runley; John Ryder; Walter Salter; Henry Sawtell; William Salsbee; Thomas Saul;(?) Jasper, Morris and Margery Smith; Nicholas and Robert Snethen; Mary Southick; Thomas, and Mirabel Stevens; Wm. Charles Stiger; Thomas Stiles; Richard Stocton, John Talman; Samuel Tatem; Dr. Henry Taylor; John and Robert Terry; Simon Thewall(?); Richard Tindal; Henry and John Townsend; Joseph, Samuel, William Jr., and John, Sr. and Jr., Thorne; Phillip Udal; Edec. Van Skyagg;(?) Ellen Wall; Wm. Warde; Richard Weller; James and Thomas Whittaker; Richard Wieday; Edec. Wilday;(?) Thomas Willde; Col. Thos. Willet; Thos. Williams; Martin Wiltse; George, David, Henry and Jona., Sr. and Jr., Wright; William, Thomas and John Yeates.

---

Analysis of the Chalybeate Mineral Spring, on the farm of Gen. Edward W. Bradley, Whitestone Avenue.

One gallon contains the following ingredients:

| | | |
|---|---|---|
| Chloride of Sodium | 1.45 | Sulphate of Lime ... .12 |
| Chloride of Calcium } | .81 | Sulpate of Soda } ... .70 |
| Chloride of Magnesium } | | Sulphate of Magnesia } |
| Bicarbonate of Magnesia | 1.08 | Organic matter ... .32 |
| Bicarbonate of Lime | .86 | Silicia, Alumnia, &c ... .14 |
| Protocarbonate of Iron | 3.20 | |

Grains, 8.86
Free Carbonic Acid, 4.268 Cubic Inches.

Some years ago the distinguished Dr. Samuel L. Mitchell, of New York, drew public attention to this water. In 1852, James R. Chilton, M. D, the well known Chemist, remarked, after the analysis of the water:—"This is a purely tonic water, and commends itself to the attention of medical men having patients under their charge who require the invigorating effects of Iron, when administered in its most efficient state of combination."

MOUNT VERNON FUND.

Received, New York April 27th, 1849, of Miss. Isabel C. Potts, of Flushing, L. I. (the appointed Lady Manager of that town) Three hundred and four dollars and three cents, being the full amount collected by her towards the "Mount Vernon Fund" as per subscription book this day returned to the office.

ELIZABETH J. MONTGOMERY, *Secretary*,

$304 03.                                                    for M. M. Hamilton.

---

## DIRECTORY OF THE VILLAGE OF FLUSHING.

*Auctioneers.*—Charles P. Lowree and Coles W. White.

*Ambrotypists.*—Seabrook E. Willett and Sylvester Roe.

*Bakers.*—John S. Pittman, M. Caveny. F. Thorp, Walter Schenk, Ira Ellis and Mrs. Wright.

*Barbers.*—William Howard and F. Klages.

*Bell Hanger*—Aslop Lawrence, who is also a Locksmith and Gunsmith.

*Blacksmiths and Wagon Makers*—George Van Ostrand, Alexander Parks, James Keefe, —— Thorn and Joseph Wright.

*Boots and Shoes.*—Jacob Roemer, Van Ostrand & Cornell, Henry Warner, John Griffin, Wilson Mitchell, Pearsall Wright, John Fleming, John Flinn and Lawrence Mahar.

*Boat Builder*—A. Hamilton.

*Building Materials*—Isaac Peck & Son, Peck & Fairweather and George B. Roe & Co.

*Cartmen.*—Thomas Farrington, Thomas Webb, Robert Smith, Squire Smith, Robert Roe, John Kelly, Peter Hade, and others.

*Carpenters and Builders.*—William Post, Benj. L. Fowler, Ebenezer West, Silvester Roe, Thomas L. Robinson, David T. Waters and Wm. Van Ostrand.

*Clothier.*—D. Masters.

*Confectionery.*—Caleb Smith, Mrs. Quarterman, and others.

*Coal, Wood, &c.*—Isaac Peck & Son, Peck & Fairweather and Wm. Hamilton & Son.

*Dentists.*—Dr Fredericks and Dr. Dodge

*Dress and Cloak Making.*—Mrs. Johnson, Mrs. Lewis, Miss Stretch, Miss Wright and Miss Todd.

*Drugs and Medicines.*—Clement & Bloodgood, Dr. C. H. Hedges.

*Dry Goods, Groceries, &c.*—Isaac Peck & Son, Alfred C. Smith, Peck & Fairweather, Clement & Bloodgood, Benj. Griffin, I. V. A. Paynter, C. Lever, James Ewbank & Son, Patrick Darcy, P. Delehanty, Samuel Foster, Thorn Smith, James Mimnaugh, Stephen Lee, Abigail Brown, James O'Brien, Walter Tobin, Richard Owen, Andrew Ryan, W. S. Bragaw, and others.

*Expresses.*—Church's Express, George Foster; Flushing Express, W. B. Conklin.

*Florists.*—Patrick Darcy, James Dent and George Johnston.

*Fancy Work.*—Mrs. C. Lever, teaches embroidery, stamping and various kinds of fancy work.

*Furniture*—Ernest Kreig. Samuel W. Fowler.

*Flour and Feed.*—Wm. Henry Roe, Wm Hamilton & Son.

*Gas Fitter.*—Richard Wallace.

*Hardware*—Eglee & Scott.

*Hats and Caps.*—P. T. Smith.

*Hotels.*—Flushing Pavilion, John Mahar; Flushing Hotel, Isaac Edwards; Farmers and Mechanics Hall, C. P. Lowerre; Deutches Hotel, C. Weber.

*Harness Makers.*—Richard Cornell, Ebenezer A. Lewis and B. Zuzi.

*Hides and Fat.*—Quinby & Field.

*Insurance*—Coles W. White and George C. Baker.

*Law.*—George W. Ralph, Charles Van Nostrand and B. W. Downing.

*Livery Stables*—William Sammis, Augustus G Boerum, Wilson E. Lawrence and Charles E. Hunt.

*Markets*—George Pople, E R. Byrd, Patrick Clark, Thomas Dowling, Van Velsor & Gildersleeve, Thomas J. Quarterman and William Stanton, deal in Poultry and Vegetables.

*Masons and Builders*—Corns W. Howard, Edward F. Smith, Hendrickson Jarvis, Addison Smith, James Carroll, Henry S. Barto and C. Powell.

*Marble and Stone Yards*—George Weaver and Daniel McCormack.

*Mineral Waters.*—Samuel B. Nicholls.

*Millinery*—Mrs. E. P Van Velsor, Mrs. Marshall & Mrs. Jane Gilligan

*Music.*—William Baldwin.

*Nurseries.*—Wm. R. Prince & Co , King & Ripley, Parsons & Co., Daniel Higgins, George D. Kimber and A. G. Silliman.

*Painters.*—James Quarterman & Sons, Richard Sanders, Edwin Hitchins, Thomas Gosling and J. Wm Quarterman.

*Periodicals*—J. B Stillwaggon, dealer in periodicals and newspapers.

*Physicians.*—Abraham Bloodgood, C. H. Hedges, C. P. Leggett, J. W. Barstow, Joseph H. Vedder, C. M. Allin and C. Strauch.

*Printers.*—C. R Lincoln and W. R. Burling.

*Real Estate Agents*—Willett & Carll.

*Restaurant.*—John Reed.

*Road Contractors.*—Henry French and John Leonard.

*Sash and Blindmakers*—John H. Lowerre and Samuel D. Smith.

*Schools.*—Flushing Institute for boys. Mrs. S. K. Roberts, and Rev. H. Dana Ward's for girls; Miss Blake & Miss. Field for young children.

*Scroll Sawing.*—Geo. A. Stillwaggon and Thomas L. Robinson.

*Segars.*—Capt. M. Morrow, importer of Havanas, and Wm. Burk.

*Seedman*—G. R. Garretson.

*Steam Mill.*—James Milnor Peck & Co., all kinds of planing and mouldings, turning, and kindling wood.

*Stoves and Tin Ware*—Eglee & Scott, Thomas Elliott, Thomas O. Morton, John Higgins and Benj. Field.

*Surveying.*—John F. Carll.

*Tailors.*—Edmund Howard, John Rickey, William Knighton and George Hemsley.

*Umbrellas and Furrier.*—J. Skinner.

*Undertakers*—Samuel W. Fowler and Seth T. Cook.

*Upholsterer.*—D. Laedein.

*Watches and Jewelry.*—Henry Carpenter and Samuel Carpenter

www.ingramcontent.com/pod-product-compliance
Lightning Source LLC
Chambersburg PA
CBHW030546040726
47497CB00008B/2593